LIMBERLOST

LIMBERLOST

by

Ricky Dale

DIADEM BOOKS

LIMBERLOST

Published by Diadem Books
Distribution coordination by Spiderwize

For information, please contact:

Diadem Books
16 Lethen View
Tullibody
ALLOA
FK10 2GE
Scotland UK

www.diadembooks.com

ISBN: 978-1-908026-13-2

To Kim and Gareth

A Note from the Author

I s *Limberlost* an innocuous place of security (a place to hide) in the consciousness of the mind—a place that succours and reconditions our psyche when we blaze a befuddled path? Or is *Limberlost* perhaps merely a suggestion of our enigmatic perception and surmised optimism?

During the last five years I have been deeply immersed in attempting to descriptionise and mimic (quite often with uncomfortable candour) the spiritual, physical and intensely personal 'Limberlost' of a unique musicologist.

The reason that my long-standing and exhausting undertaking has been somewhat delicate and ticklish is because it became necessary to research through the empathy, dreamtime, and reflection of my protagonist.

By virtue of her patience, I am finally confidant and qualified to release this novel in the undaunted knowledge that it is an honourable picture of the 'voice'.

CHAPTER 1

The sky was uncaring, motionless, and heavy with snow. She lowered her eyes to the magazine on her lap and flicked carelessly and obliviously through the glossy pages. The Greyhound tyres began their journey, scorching methodically through the shivering white debris.

It was the coldest and worst winter since '52, and time had been a marathon as she cautiously navigated her path through the erratic white-out of error and truth. Slipping and sliding, she tottered across Maple Street toward Brant; cruelly clothed in her emptiness and the shabby secrets that no one should ever guess or know about.

Her crumpled luggage of precious meagre possessions were hiding cluttered in an unwieldy mundane Towers holdall; clinging to and strangling her frozen fingers: like the numbed remain it was.

There had always been an obtrusive line between the fantasy and the reality of her life; at last it had finally changed; no longer was it the glaring blinding blur of her own misguided idealism.

Her voice; a vibrant explosive force; a virtuoso, who eclipsed all conventional so-called musical sense and expression; a prodigy of such calibre to create individual definitive parallels. There was no way to explain her genius, but in every way they had recognized it; mercilessly.

It had seemed like her summer of discovery, and it was: her aspirations versus their objectives. A commodity of their trade, she was ideal manageable manipulation: enthusiastic and excited; submissive and powerless; they were her impresarios of insanity, ready to applaud, or to be in at the kill.

Before the bouquets of red roses had dropped, the glitzy entertainment machine of coercion and subtle intimidation had been set in motion; pushing her forward, preventing her from escape.

Her voice, desperate and eager to live; abused and interlocked with heart-gouging heavy roles sung too soon: clamouring to be heard; desiring to indulge and gratify demanding and beguiled audiences.

It was a vocal agony too unbearable to watch. She had become mentally encapsulated in a walking coma; like another person watching herself. Singing at the top of her voice; challenging herself; testing herself; sweeping everything before her. Unlike her voice, her sapping strength was not so perfectly deluded.

She could hear clearly the sobs of injured stretched and exhausted nerves and longed for the mettle to 'walk-away'; it was as though the humiliation was a personal jailer and trauma her only reprieve.

With arms tired from reaching out to touch, she plummeted in a blaze of flash bulbs; her voice trembling and silent, words muffed, sinuses chocked, her nadir unclad.

The awe-inspiring princess had especially held her audience in the late editions; they were on the lookout for weaknesses and had not allowed her to get away with anything; although Toronto Free Press had printed her a spectacular obituary of Emily Dickinson's "WILL THERE REALLY BE A MORNING!"

With their source of income frayed she was jettisoned like unwelcome wreckage; consigned and misplaced to any neighbourhood unsung three piece combo, who frequent one or some downtown Dream Street eatery, or uptown basement bar.

The sombre afternoon shadows were creeping lazily across the motel drapes. She sat silently, mesmerized by the hollow void: each larynx whimper succeeded by a shiver: each stab of disappointment followed by a shambolic shrug.

A bitter taste crossed her lips; it was judgement time; the infinite finale; her neglected decision was at last conclusive: -

No more scattered weeping lyrics to bemused drunks or loud conversationalists whilst a piano is worthlessly thumped!

No more seedy crap game bars and fast-eat emporiums, where spectators and performers jostle through the same wash rooms! No more self-styled friends and importunate bums and cadgers by the grease load. No more sleazy lawyers with worthless investments; or theatrical dykes and depraved agents who are eager to become paternal and 'look-after' the naïve and the floundering!

She had seen it, and seen through it; and there is nothing as sordid and sad as a singer who still believes in becoming a great star once again, purely because it suits their inclinations and dreams.

She lifted her heavy head from the magazine, gazed dreamily through the tinted glass of the bus, and out into the neon lit night. She felt unreal, like an actress in some silent movie who is waiting for applause from a non-existing audience. She was emotionally sick by the contemptuous inimical deceit. They had made her become a shadow of a shadow, a disguise of the person that she once was.

Here in the wings as the curtains dropped she was struck by the realization that just maybe she had the chance to make an exit and finally break free. Perhaps her life may surface again through her cold, damaged psyche. Her conscience was already beating with thunderous applause from the moral sense that had been suffocated and dormant, and was now surfacing through her wounds of stigma. She felt an emancipation to be out of that stagnant spotlight and never would again succumb to be someone's pitiful lean-to, or join the melancholy queue of the crushed. The false face and switched on hair that had made her become the obsession of quick-buck hunters from flesh bound backgrounds, were yesterday's popcorn.

She breathed the cigarette smoke in deeply and collected her thoughts like a large sum of money. She, the dejected, demeaned heroine had finally accomplished bitter fame, she had become the revolutionary, the subversive, and now, detached. Her life had disguised itself with hoaxed professionalism, but the truth was always known to its victim.

Cedar and jagged fir passed by. She loved this Greyhound, steadfast on its rails of pity, taking her faraway from yesterday's memory of bruises and lies. She watched the austere trees transparent against the infinity of the falling snow and watery twilight... flicking by as sleep devoured her.

CHAPTER 2

A truck with loose chains was clanking rhythmically, waking her from soft oblivion. She watched the creased passengers embarking at the half-stage terminus and began to follow them out into the glassy iceland.

The midnight restaurant casts its spectrum of light warmly and reassuringly. she had a favourable anticipation about this hospitable oasis. She sat alone and felt a certain apprehension about being alone. This was the first solitary interval of her journey. She had no idea of her expectations, or if the next bend in the road offered a home coming; although she was not really wishful of such.

Through the plate glass windows, she watched the forest fade as the snow became denser and in an optimistic burst decided that even this remote place was an improvement on some mean tavern on Yonge Street. Reflections of the existence that she had been trapped in, already began to feel shrouded. She had always taken the wrong turn but perhaps lost in this trackless forest, the present may scribble over the past. Perchance the winter moon may warm her cool heart once more.

In an enormous size 60 overall the remarkably nimble waiter floated toward her like a marauding balloon. As he came abruptly to a standstill, she detected a screech; which she hoped appertained to his plimsolls and not flatulence! He began to recite the first forty chapters of the menu and specials, which was followed by a huge enquiring smile, and silence. Feeling like a tap dancer apologizing for a fall, she was quietly embarrassed to meagrely order coffee and reserve a cabin.

A young boy with an Elvis quiff, clownish smile and ungainly stride, escorted her across the frozen picnic ground toward the cabin. She had noticed him earlier amusing himself with a scrawny black cat, which he now carried with unwieldiness under his coat. The cabin lay several hundred yards from the restaurant retreating submissively on the bank of a frozen creek, and converging upon uncultivated woodland. Brushwood had gathered around the threshold of the entrance door and the huge pines creaked and moaned in the pitiless wind, and dropped their needles noisily upon the roof.

The accommodation was sparse but nevertheless it was clean and homely: a huge iron bed stood like a formidable fortress in the centre of the room, flanked by a large dresser and several overstuffed chairs; in the corner the Frigidaire was humming a requiem to an untroubled ancient potbelly wood stove. This was a practical and sensible place, a remnant of the past, but a retreat with sympathy that welcomed travellers looking for defection and sanctuary. She made coffee and sat huddled, clasping the mug as though it was the stone face of a lover. Her tears dropped full and involuntary as she watched the snow pile itself against the steely windowpanes. Each flake obscuring and hiding her from the bleak reality of the outside world, blanketing and pervading her mind with security, from the fearsome anonymous faces that had encroached upon her sanity.

That literal yesterday of meaninglessness, purposelessness and normlessness; if there ever was a norm it was abnormality.

CHAPTER 3

M orning came and the hemlocks of danger seemed to have distanced themselves. No fan mail today but it was good to be letter lonely. Recently there were only two or three letters each month in any event. She had once been the recipient of several long distance telephone calls from a miner in Thunder Bay. Whilst on a visit to Toronto he had seen her perform and had telephoned her every time he was intoxicated.

The thermometer on the outer cabin wall was down to ten degrees Fahrenheit. It had stopped snowing and the virgin snow lay like a dessert that could be eaten with cream and sugar; she had once read where it was really good to eat that way. There was no friction in colours this time of the year, it was a pure snowy-eyed country.

Feeling ridiculous in her court shoes, she carefully treaded her way like a foal with its nose in the grass, toward the dapper little restaurant.

The proprietor of impropriety, and maître d' of mellifluous charisma, was a silvered hair mom hen; who inescapably was charming and alarming the early morning truckers with her amusing banter. Those all-nighters, eyes glazed with frost, they needed and revelled in this bunkhouse talk and motherly attention. When the guys pulled the strings, their protagonist would score back with a collection of bilingual garbage; it was haute cuisine at its very finest!

The door made an apologetic creak as she entered, and they turned around and glanced at her as though she has just emerged from some thicket. After a minute or two of silence, they happily began to stampede back into their hot and full-throated exchange again.

Escaping sheepishly into the shelter of a booth, she carelessly flicked through the jukebox itinerary, and coaxed a smile at the countless 50's timeworn oldies; the desire for updated melody had obviously eluded evolution here in the sticks. Time has its ends and its beginnings and they were content with the familiar, and not swayed to new drumbeats yet.

'You look as pale as tears girl, the worse case of dehydration I ever saw.' Apple cheeked mom, bundled up in her mohair cardigan was crouched on one knee beside her. Like a mother mops an infant's nose she added, 'Not goin' to ask you what you want, goin' to fetch you what you need.'

With her starched petticoats scuffling like crisp autumn leafs, mom disappeared into her kitchen kingdom; leaving behind her a redolence of cigarette smoke and peppermint creams. She sat, hands clasped on her lap, motionless and serene. She seemed caught between time past and time present, broken by strength and yet still strong. She smiled wistfully; kindness, nay tenderness was so hard to swallow.

She thought of the falling snow the night before. It can take a town at night and its muffle, and it had taken her too. The unlanterned darkness and shadows had been dispelled in its whiteness; the wetness of her eyes were no longer tears, merely snow flakes melting upon her face. Patiently waiting for her return, a silent door had slowly opened; the inarticulate murmurs of nowhere sadness no longer reached toward her.

CHAPTER 4

S he drifted in a dream of obliviousness along the bank of Winter Creek; it came around a bend above, disappeared around a bend below, and was filled to the brim with snow. This was her private Eden; the sky an intense azure; the sun had foiled winters plan today; even the trees stood motionless as if they dare not stir, lest it should break the ominous silence. Locked in her thoughts she was barely aware of someone coming in her direction.

He appeared to be whispering into the physiological kingdom that surrounded him and also seemed heedless to her presence. Draped in murky denims and caribou-skins he dragged a lame leg, like a dying phoenix, through the broken skeletons of pinewood. His grainy grip clenched a hatchet but not in a fearsome or intimidating manor; people are made of places, and nature had defined this extension in sympathy.

He stopped several yards away from her. Although his face was half hidden by long black hair, she could still detect a question on his lips and in his saddened face; because the answer had become indelible. A renegade and nomad, his home amid a wilderness of trees. How short a period in the page of time that the tribes imagined us in their future, but we never imagined them in our past.

He broke the solemn silence like a warm wind across fields of snow, 'our tracks cohabit', he drawled. Her attention was completely engulfed and she was unable to conceal her concentrated stare. Her mind whirled wordlessly, she waited expectantly; and thought fruitlessly about her neglected make up and weary white skin. She trembled, but not with anxiety, only anticipation. He added, 'I see you are afraid of yourself'. With an ash taste in her mouth she hesitated momentarily, and smiling she replied. 'You know my secret'. There was an equipoise of calm between them erasing pretence and doubt. Several moments where time is suppressed and a gift is given of a journey through a lifetime. A gift so special, that it is a way through one another, and the beginning is at the end of now. He had come to her in solitude and as they met themselves coming round again the dream had run its course and dissolved into reality.

He unlocked his voice and said, 'I see a tree that is greater than all the others, but the cones for my fire are beyond reach'. Their eyes met in recognition; he took a step forward and stumbled slightly, and like an anonymous passer by who had returned a lost child to its mother, he was passing past her.

In the evening, she gazed through her cabin window, across Winter Creek and could see the flickering glow from his firelight; maybe even a glimpse of his dark shape silhouetted.

In the snowy stillness, he had given her absolution of a kind, and now the sight of his fire made the nothingness become bearable.

She watched the easy wind blowing a few downy flakes around and recalled their encounter; of how she had stood in the shade of his shadow, whilst their minds skated upon the silver creek.

CHAPTER 5

Her pillow welcomed her that night. Watching the winter moon's tranquil light filtering through the latticed panes, she drifted into the evanescence of slumber.

Her serenity was abruptly broken by a muffled hubbub and activity outside the cabin. Rising from bed and tightening her wrap, she stepped cautiously toward the door. She was aware that it was bad judgement to venture outside alone at night; but the isolation of this place did not bother her; and in any event, she was inclined to being inquisitive.

Stepping outside against the sting of the north wind her watery eyes captured a beautiful shadowy creature foraging amorously and painstakingly through the spent garbage. Like an unwelcome guest, she retreated determinedly backwards. Likewise, her visitor's liquid eyes panicked and instinctively it bolted; more like a headstrong horse than a wolf; straight without veering into its forest sanctuary. She had seen traces of paws dappling the ashen ground the day before, but had no idea that she would meet the perpetrator. She smiled to think that for one brief moment nature was changeless, and yet fundamentally their existence interlocked; for like her it had run from the crooked world. Accidents do happen to your soul in a place like this, after destiny has fortuitously melted your tracks.

CHAPTER 6

Winter finally compromised to spring, and although spring was unpunctual it was making up for lost time. One smiling morning the birds were invited to sing the message of summer and the rich-petaled orange blossom began to scatter life back into nature's complexion.

There was breath and warm pulsations throughout the pinelands. Each orphaned cypress stood taller and more dauntless against its newly preened inhabitants. The ice in Winter Creek had melted into a glare of sunlight, and its banks were overflowing with exuberant flora. At night, the gossip crickets with their small innumerable voice, clasped the night air and extinguished the silence. The vast star-embroidered sky gazed down and proudly announced the supreme diadem of existence to all that murmurs and dwells.

Such is the character of seasons in this clime. There is an obvious absence of mellifluous wooing; when a season decides its voice has become subdued, the ensuing season is waiting to conceive, and quickly descents.

CHAPTER 7

S he had ventured to the restaurant for provisions and the like on various occasions. Her visits had been brief although from time to time; when she felt more self-assured, she would sit for a spell and indulge herself with moms coconut cream or pumpkin pie alamode. Mom seemed perceptive to her need for obscurity and never probed or queried her solitary withdrawal. Although the past months had fleetingly slipped through her fingers, she did not regard them as wasted or indeed that she may have fallen into a rut; on the contrary she had enjoyed her privacy. She had taught herself to live simply and was content for her voice to be silent. There had been times when she felt insecure, this would occur in the evening or late at night when her self- esteem would dwindle to zero; but the early mornings she adored. To rise early and to be the first person breathing the dawns cold breath, and the intoxicating feeling of seemingly being the only one awake in a world wrapped in sleep. From time to time the bad memories did repeat, but not so much to care, and today she felt eager to cast away winter's sombre attire in total emancipation. Her heart fluttered in apprehension as she made her way through the stubbled grass toward the restaurant.

The exuberant boy was swinging precariously on a rope that he had attached to a ragged branch; each sweeping movement was carrying him further across Winter Creek.

As she approached, he stopped tentatively slid down the rope, and stood gazing at her intently. 'Hi kid, watch out for the turtles', she said jestfully. She was surprised by her tête-à-tête and at how buoyant her voice sounded. Squinting sideways, away from the glare of the sunlight, he replied 'What's yorn name, and where you come from?'

She was noticeably taken unaware; at least it seemed that way to her. A faraway look came into her eyes and she replied softly 'I belong to my mother ... or to nobody or everyone. but you can call me whatever you wish'. In an unexpected display of concern and tenderness. he reached out assuringly squeezed her hand gently, and temperately responded 'I will collect some names for you'.

Her eyes smiled at him, it was as though he understood that her heart was a profoundly secret place.

CHAPTER 8

Derived from Greek ancestry, George the chicken farmer was tall, lean and proud. The unhalting bastard furrows upon his mummified face and his battered wooden farmhouse were a honest testimony of endurance and defiance against the ferocity of many hostile seasons. He was a well-loved character and local folk would tease him by quipping how they could smell his property as they passed it by on the highway. George enjoyed the jocularity and would make a big toothless grin and retort that it was the smell of work. He was a lonely person, and their humour indicated that at least they were thinking about him. For years, he had become a habitual diner at Moms, doubtless because the companionship was more desirable than several hundred chickens clucking about aimlessly.

At the sight of her entering the restaurant, he leapt to attention in polite welcome, and in his fractured English declared, 'to be silent is not to fraternize, so will you please permit to join me and we'll decide what crust is to be discovered today.' She noticed how distinguished he looked; his faded blue suit (complete with frayed vest), which he had obviously worn for this occasion; and how his eyes, unaccustomed to shade still squinted from habit; but most of all the plea contained in them. She smiled gracefully and replied, 'I would be delighted, sir.' She sat opposite him and his face beamed with gratitude as he complimented. 'I notice you here several times, you have good clothes, even into the accustom of wearing good clothes.' He surprised her because her own eyes had forgotten to see her.

For precious moments they laughed and eat in each other's direction, and chased the nakedness of lonely away from cracked sidewalks to warm beaches. Although their eyes had taken them

15

beyond, time was beginning to dissolve; with a glimmer of mischievousness on his face, he announced, 'I am indebted that you have taken nourishment with me, your lungs stir the leaves and ruffle my twilight'. Reflecting seriously for a moment, he added, 'If God can strike down butterflies and then change rain to rainbows, I am happy that He has stopped the fire you lived in.'

An encounter with a stranger and yet he had viewed her page of desolation, and only spoken when he knew that she had forgotten the last word on that page. Watching her circle back through the maze, he had understood, and he had welcomed her back.

CHAPTER 9

O ne smiling morning, that breathing spring, time forgot how far
she had journeyed to be here. Here at her own pace, here in her
own moments. That smiling morning, she impulsively chose this
moment to confront the three-mile walk in order to look over the local
village.

Anville was far removed from the continuity of modern life and
was happy to remain that way; uninterrupted, rejecting the unfamiliar
as though it was unnecessary to investigate.

Its wide, tree-shaded street stretched from one end of the town to
the other. At the extreme end was open farming country, and at the
near end stood the ramshackle railway station. The wooden sidewalks,
broken in places by pushing roots of trees, ran along side an
insignificant parade of weary stores and then halted abruptly. Apart
from the Bank and Barber Shop, folks mainly visited town for the
General Store where, if you cared to forage through the socks, ear
warmers and the like, you would pretty well find anything you
required.

She strolled into town with a collection of dust and small stones in
her shoes, stopping to shake her shoes she could feel the stillness and
calm in the humid air. It was as though the day had no option but to
drop nonchalantly by. Glancing questioningly at her passing reflection
in a store window, she decided recklessly that it was time to shed her
old identity and preen the new. Determined, but with her heart
captured in apprehension, she entered Toni's Barber Shop and
enquired, 'Will you cut my hair... I would like you to cut my hair...
short... please, if you will.' Toni stood positively immobile, muted

words staggered in silence from his mouth, and time looked like it was tapping even more rapidly upon his quizzically ruckled brow.

Eventually he mustered all his ardour together and gushed, 'The last week of August 62, at the Sheraton, an artist performed Curuso. I watched your voice, it was so beautiful, I hoped I would never smile again. When the eyes cry, is nothing, you made my soul cry.'

CHAPTER 10

S he fritted away the hours rummaging through interesting bric-a-brac at the thrift shop and trading post, and when her curiosity began to wane, she commenced to make her way home. Feeling detached and aloof from baneful constriction, she felt ready to dream nice things again. Strolling past the railway station and out onto the overgrown roadside grass which led out of Anville, she quickened her step toward the restaurant. The walk was pleasant and she felt a happy anticipation as she rounded the bend and saw her adopted home in the clearing.

Trucks and convertibles littered the drive-in and the air was awake with lively music from the jukebox. The picnic tables were swarming with carefree families and several youngsters were gathering wild flowers and berries and wading in Winter Creek. She could eavesdrop on folks with thick soft southern accents and recognized many local folks who were making up for the long hard winter. The restaurant was alive and breathing and embraced its patrons with a love obeyed and relished.

Intuitively and without a moment's hesitation she gathered up a tray of dregs and greasy plates and bee-lined toward the kitchen. Mom was in automatic mode, she had delegated apprentices of every persuasion, peeling potatoes, washing dishes and waiting table. It transpired that the local baseball team had requisitioned themselves!

Mom had a 'we share, we care' kinship with 'her boys'. They were not merely customers or friends, they were her family. They came to swallow a refreshing river of Cola and such, but the restaurant was teeming and their mom had coping difficulties; en masse, they became her pinch[1] hitters. This was their dug out,[2] their home.

'What have you done to your hair', mom remarked sternly. After pausing for several moments for an explanatory reply she added sadly, 'you had such beautiful hair'.

She smiled at mom shamefully and replied 'I wanted to get rid of my shroud'. Throwing another T-bone onto the grill mom retorted 'The ballerina has become a street car driver'. She smiled wistfully, she knew that mom's frozen observation was not a scorn. it was simply the way of affirming her heart.

Whitie, the team's captain, came lurching through the kitchen swing doors with a precariously held mountain of grimy plates and a sweat-wet shirt. His face gleamed as she reached to recover the plates from him, and with bland serenity, he blurted. 'The girl I never met, hi, Toni told me about you'. She froze, afraid to speak, like an ardent fan he gushed 'Would you sing at our barn dance?' The shock quickly passed, and although she realised that his impromptu adolescent banter was only welcoming kindness, she was nevertheless amazed and numbed at how word can spread so quickly in a small community.

Shortly after 6 pm, the afternoon began to cool and shadow into evening. She had enjoyed the day and respectfully got through it, although the encounters and the brand new questions had made her nervous.

Unexpectedly she was feeling a certain happy experimentation with her newfound freedom, but she was still between a life just past and a just beginning. She wanted so much to reach beyond her three-octave voice; it was as though she was singing a duet to herself but that the other voice was an orphan and missing in her throat. She wanted to sing again and perhaps with a little effort she could make it so, but for now she would sing only for her; no one would ever command her mouth again.

---

[1] A substitute batter
[2] Area where players sit when not actively engaged on the pitch

History would not repeat itself, if indeed it were a challenge that she might accept. She would decide where to begin. and it would not be in a search for impresarios or for the sounds of winters past.

Like a sparrow who has learned the serenade and left its nest, the choice and the offering would be hers.

CHAPTER 11

I t was hot, an incandescent curtain of rabid sultriness. The humidity was inflamed and grey clouds had piled themselves upon the curdling sun. Far off in the southwest thunder rolled in dwindling intervals.

With one leg curled under her, she sat at a picnic table enjoying iced tea and casually watching customers to-ing and fro-ing the restaurant.

A '54 pickup glided by and honked, she waved back; it was George smiling a large toothless grin. She pulled a pack of Camel from the pocket of her jeans and flicked the Zippo into flame, compiling her thoughts and gazing contently across the fallow summer meadows; this place of certainty, this anchored home that had unexpectedly welcomed her from the edge of nowhere.

She tilted back her head and finished the tea, snuffed out her cigarette in the ashtray and walked through the staggering tufts of grass toward the restaurant.

Her absence from life had been rewarding to her repose, but life was reopening and it was time to do something; she desired to become involved, and it was true that mom needed seasonal help. It was as though an evolution had drawn slowly and faithfully upon her, and along with the reflex of spring, she had given distance to those graven images of the past.

The big fans on the ceiling were whirring and although the restaurant door was open, the hubbub from the jukebox seemed to make the salty people look hotter than it really was; a foreshadowed storm always had a confused nebulous effect in this region.

Mom was sat at the counter, talking in an aura of hilarity and a haze of smoke; it was as though she was unaware that the restaurant was pretty much brimful. It was mom's philosophy to keep the tourists feeding and fed, and the coffee freshly brewed, the interim period was her prelude to amuse. They say that people are made of places but this place was made of mom; this restaurant was her curious and eccentric land. It contained her personality, each brick, each segment invoked her pleasure and her pain. As she entered mom was sat with her back to her. Without turning and as if by some incredulous sixth sense, she waved her arm and beckoned: 'Darling, come and sit with me and tell me things.'

She gazed at mom and her confidence began to wane and betray her. Her vocabulary was dissolving in her throat, her limbs felt heavy and lethargic; only her ability to tremble reminded her that she was at all extant. To her credit, she had not changed her mind, and the emptiness in her head pronounced her even more pathetic. It was never this complicated to walk on stage, all that required was a firm coolness; and yet to play the part of hired hand was her toughest role yet. To return to life, one needs an approach, it need not be intricate but it requires an arrangement of words to cause a happening, any approach would suffice... her stammering eyes supplicated her pleading words and beseeching expression, each echoing but silent as though a conspiracy held them together.

Mom was a woman of bare instincts and earth words; she realised how much guts it took for her to come even this far and had seen the convulsions of despair when she arrived that bleak winter night. She knew how she had been crying in the dark yet sleeping with her eyes open in fear, playing solitaire with flawed and broken dreams. Only yesterday, she had understood the motive behind her cut and ragged mane. She could read the voice that was enquiring through delicate sad eyes.

Mom spoke with defined gentleness. 'From where I sit, time smoothes and fills, smoothes and fills, sometimes the traffic through that door is backed up for miles, but you could be my sunbeam from out of the snow, cause I need a reflection of myself here'.

She was backing into the world with a quickening start and enthusiastically replied, 'Mom, I'm a pure blood domestic, guaranteed!'

Mom perused her face with concern 'you carried your grief alone, a fool flaunts it, but you hemmed it in. You are a noble girl, and beauty is what beauty does.'

CHAPTER 12

I t was 6am and the morning had just opened its eyelids. The air was fresh and green with the scent of dewed grass and fir trees.

Today her heart and soul were dressed in spotless attire, since this especial morning was unequal to any other; it oozed with concealed expectations.

The restaurant was still draped in a hue of mist; looking and feeling elegant, she stepped outside her cabin, breathed deeply, and raced briskly and gracefully toward her new vocation.

She recognized an analogy between being a vocalist and the language of her come-lately occupation. Often a person's presence means more to the audience than the song, naturally the singer needs a special gift to achieve this. Mom had that special gift, she wanted it, and was determined to aspire to obtain it. In the event that her new endeavour and private life were united, perhaps aftermost, she would become the flower that had found its perfume on both sides.

Mom greeted her with a sprightly voice 'Coffee or orange juice, dear'; she was busy making up the specials for the day. 'We've got a family coming in from the boondocks shortly, they are as dirty as a ducks puddle, guess it's going to be an initiation that will certainly show you where the bear stood in the buckwheat. They come in for an early breakfast every several months; guess we're their special treat. The father's so thin, I've seen more meat on a hockey stick, and the mother is pure beef to the ankles. Lots of kids, good kids, except when they are shooting bunnies!'[3]

---

[3] breaking wind

CHAPTER 13

With pistons rising and plunging in grumbling pain, the hued green Dodge rolled cautiously onto the gravelled drive-in.

She noticed an array of happy faces on the many hardy little individuals that were bundled under coats and blankets in the open trailer. As the truck groaned to a halt, they began to spill out in a jumble of skirts and shirts. She counted at least six kids, but maybe eight; all their haste and commotion seemed to have given them an ability to reinvent their numbers! In a harmony of bodies they came, squeezing and forcing themselves through the entrance door. The calamity was even more conspicuous because it was an uproar of complete silence; through all the wrestling and jockeying for position, not one child uttered a word. Pa stepped firmly from the cab, adjusted his suspenders and strolled almost motionlessly around the perimeter of the truck; seemingly checking if anything had dropped off! He opened the passenger door for Ma and the vehicle bowed its incline as she eased herself out onto the running board. Majestically and with fingers locked together, as if this was their bridal days honeymoon, they dignifyingly entered the restaurant.

She was somewhat aghast, certainly surprised and definitely out of her element. This somewhere of humanness that made it so obvious that she had been looking at the world upside down; this is not the way it was in the city. These people are bearers of a message from a different world; a world where the tiny atomies of life are bred and understood, where perfection and innocence still clasp a halcyon ray, and the truth of flesh and spirit sing together, all in tune.

She hurried to their table, the plaintive waitress with tarnished souvenirs, alive with a new expectation this 'host' family had unwittingly given her.

Without fuss and fanfare, Pa quietly ordered for the family: 'We know what's for supper, going to tell you the first and last thing, to save your legs, girl.' The table quickly became a tempting island of food, which was 'shared' according to the explicit meaning of the word: several kids picked upon Ma's T-Bone whilst ma poured the wild berries she had gathered into Pa's cereal. She loved and revelled in the many little aesthetics that these country folk ignored. She also learned how cola cans have a distinct musical harmony when they hit the ground simultaneously, and that Teem cans are about an octave higher!

Apart from all the guzzling and slavering they pretty much eat in silence; except for Pa interrupting a young one who was playing carelessly with some strawberry shortcake 'You may be chasing a crow for that afore next spring.'

As quickly as they arrived and after a wary glance from Pa, they disburdened themselves in unison from the debris. Pa scrutinized the restaurant and remarked apathetically, 'Full as an egg, see yous all afore winter, Lord willing and the crick don't rise.'

Restitution for the mowing of the carpet with pan and broom came with the unexpected discovery of a confetti of lazy dollar bills bequeathed under plates, cups and generally scattered over the table. She had imagined this to be payment, but it transfigured to be tips!

Unexpectedly, she had forged another alliance today; this time with the most vulnerable and fragile part of existence, the enduring spirit; hers and theirs. To all intents and purposes very different worlds, but bonded in a universal language of unpretentious simplicity.

CHAPTER 14

Although she became harnessed to her work, the lazy summer weeks were soft upon her feminine fingers. She had found a new music, a music understood only by her, and each day provided an anodyne and forgetting to the pitiless past. There were occasions when she would stare back into the darkness but they were few. Mom would often see it in her eyes and shake her with a mixture of words like coloured playing cards; not always complimentary but always like a candle lighting those dismal obscure corners. Mom introduced her to everyone, everyone that is except for an exhausted solitary character who had come billowing by shortly before Canada day.

It was around 7 am; she was watering the plants outside the rear screen-door. Her concentration was drawn toward a crackling commotion coming from the sombre dead twiggy stuff of bushes and small trees. Sprinting like an American fullback emerged an elderly bespectacled man with squinting eyes and baggy jaw line determinedly pushed out. He was closely and resolutely followed by two OPP's. This was a people chase: no vehicles smashing together, no swerving onto sidewalks or down over embankments to end in flames; just a single massive maple tree root that sent him sprawling.

She lowered her eyes briefly, unable to look at the pain in his eyes, which was quickly interceded by rage. Instinctively, she ran to his aid, but in that moment, which existed for only her and him, he whispered 'Don't give me a hand. Remember that folks giving Christ a hand got theirs nailed too.'

Like a child with confused inclinations, she stood motionless and reluctantly watched as the cops cuffed him. 'We didn't come for your autograph, why'd you run?' 'Run', he replied, 'Goddamn, I'm in training, anyhow you know I'll be back in 24 hours!'

He was the quintessential hood, an ageing Frank Nittie, cartoon swagger and all. As they bundled him into the black and white, he gave her a wink of recognition and an appreciative smile. In a tyre-burning cloud of dust, they disappeared hastily toward the city.

It transpired that he was the proprietor of the Golden Gloves Motel, some miles west of Anville. The village had closed ranks when rumours about his links with Sam Giancana and the Organization were being aired. Chicago had been running a fever of a hundred and one, what with the Joe Valachi[4] thing; but he would not give names, and so periodically, they arrested him. It was a kind of spiritual battle between him and the Law that was going nowhere.

Mom said that he had been a boxer and stunt man, and although he was known by the locals as *that sonofabitch*, she described him as a restless and reckless adventurer, who had a mastery of a particular step. 'One ahead of the cops; not too bright with maple trees, though!' she added jocularly.

---

[4] Valachi 'sang like a canary' at the Senate Investigations of '62

CHAPTER 15

It was a watery twilight, the sun and moon were dozing and the austere trees seemed to have lost all trace of themselves. A slight scent of loneliness melted in the air. The highway stood empty and the restaurant had shrugged to a standstill in a concentrated ambience of melancholy and serene detachment from the outside world.

From out of the silent solitude came a whimpering reverberation, which quickly clamoured into a roar. It was as though the conductors baton had lost its power of assertiveness as it crescendoed into a riotous bottomless pit of dark torrent that almost made the twilight shatter into fragments.

Around the bend they came, like cosmic objects, each Harley breaking down all traces of loneliness and swinging into the drive-in as though magnetically drawn toward the 'Ice Cold Coke' sign. Silence was cut by the final rev and, like harbingers announcing Brando and Dean, they merged into the restaurant in harlequin globs of black swirling colour. The girls skeetering ahead in sky-high heels and all-ass-wiggles; the guys, a fraternity of hip-swayers clothed from hair to boots in a rapture of cool.

Mom's hospitality embraced them, 'You're aspirin for my soul', she preened and turning to her she added, 'meet the *die early and avoid the fate of dying late* hell-bent guys'.

'Push the tables and chairs against the walls girl, tonight we're having a ris-sike-al', Eagles began to flood the jukebox, rock was spinning, and they were swaying and swinging. She watched mom clapping in tune as the room revolved. Music gives birth to everything and, for the living child in her, mom was ageless.

30

She gazed at them dancing uncontrollably, like pricked balloons all over the floor. A curious hurt bled through her soul, the memory of pleasure and freedom from inhibition was so dim in her mind. Not by design, she glanced and smiled warily at a mountainous blue denim clad figure who has just fed the jukebox and was slouched on a stool cleaning his nails with a switchblade. His lips curved to match her smile and he gestured to her. Despite his tough exterior, there was a look of safety and sympathy in his eyes. Her heart was pounding, her cigarette; the last refuge, had burned down to her finger, she tapped it out and felt foolish, yet impatient to respond. She was an agile and proficient dancer but had learned not to covet the past.

He looked at her restlessly. She stood up recklessly, almost startling herself by the movement. The room became frozen in limitless slow motion, and her face was scarlet flushed and ablaze. He reached out and grabbed her hand and she twilled afloat and engulfed in waves of excitement. She looked into his appeased face and laughed happily, 'this is not a bad idea.' It was as though the last tear that had hung so perilously on the fringe of her lashes had finally disappeared.

CHAPTER 16

It was around 9.30 pm; she stepped outside her cabin. The moon was full, bright and hanging above the forest like a giant Christmas light. Its ancillary Mars was glowing in conspicuous sympathy slightly below. Those unique summer nights, when the vegetation is so heavy and luxurious, and the evening air intoxicating.

She glanced across the picnic ground to the sound of voices heard coming from the long grass at the rear of the restaurant. Mom was delighting and entertaining a select audience of friends. They were some of the community's upstanding citizens and included Jim Eckers, the local cop. Jim noticed her, and beckoned her to join their group. She had more than a notion that tonight more gossip and truth would be told than Jim would ever have acquired on superfluous patrolling. She was also going to learn about mom's protected and gratefully shared secret that "lived" in the restaurant basement.

The basement was always kept locked with the secret, secrets. It was rumoured among the local kids, and perhaps some moronic adults, that Mom's mad relative dwelled down there. The semblance was that he was an English Lord named P.B.Fogwash: 'A child's imagination is an enchanting antidote to reality', mom remarked. 'We all enjoy delusion', she added with affection. Jim liked to be the philosopher and summed up by adding 'It's better for some folk to be on the outside and in the dark, than knowing, and caging them on the inside'.

The restaurant had concealed its mysterious legacy since speakeasies replaced saloons. The 'Thunder Road' runners who convoyed nightly excursions across the border into Buffalo had long since disappeared, but this had remained a dry area, and mom had kept her border 'still' functional. Although U.S. Prohibition Law went down the drain in '33, mom's original drains, where hooch could be poured in a raid, were operational. There were decades of tradition in moms basement, both the cops and the good folk were paid in liquid assets. No one attempted to resist mom's potato - brewed whiskey.

They would carry on drinking 'till half a glass became a bottle, finally two, and then the evening would start awakening. The problem was, that with every new story or encounter of hearsay, there became a new beginning, and they would meet themselves coming around again!

From time to time. the discussions would lilt toward highbrow. That night the contentment of the milieu invoked argument over the physical environment. Roy Buchannan, from the Royal Bank, reckoned he could always foreguess the announcement of winter, 'It's because of the cooler nights', he said. His wife, Marie, added with gusto, 'And the shorter days'. Mom. looking very confident and knowledgeable, declared, 'soon as I see the shades of red, crimson and golden leaves, I know that the degrees are dropping and slowing the flow of sap in the trees'. Don from the Hardware Store had been watching her intently and eventually, if not inopportunely, asked 'What's our new guests assessment of these matters?' She felt herself blush as all eyes hit upon her to be the orator. She paused and serenely replied 'I guess it's the flocks of Canada geese and ducks as they make their way south for the winter'. They all nodded in agreement; and Jim asked for his usual sobering cabin for later.

She reflected upon her answer and was somewhat amused by the juxtaposition of the birds and herself. Leaving worries and problems behind, just a flap of their wings and they are free.

CHAPTER 17

The Epilogue

Uniqueness, obsessive singularity, this morning no one was identical to her, and she was proud of it.

Although she had enjoyed depending upon her impassioned loneliness (one can get accustomed to loneliness), her pain was always an entwined reality with claws and devouring jaws. It was her own intentional and excruciating assassin. Always inside of her was a judge who had tried to remain silent, but the intention of sentencing for past recriminations would always be imposed upon herself. She was never guilty in any event, but had nevertheless blamed herself far better than anyone else could. It had become so difficult to dispel the taste of resignation; the excrement of hatred was always lingering real and dormant in the wings.

Here she was lying in the grass of memory that was becoming overgrown and overcome by flowers and butterflies but she could not subdue the rancid history of the past. She was allowing it to become her burden of the present. This new life that had created itself, outside of her, but with her in mind, it had transformed her; but the special moments when her body felt exuberant, when it loved to forget itself, and would fly beyond all limits of happiness that she could ever have imagined, were few and short lived.

There was a law of cause and effect that applied to everything and everybody endeared to her. The hatred of her past life's foolishness had manifested itself in the cruellest way. She had become the self-drowning woman, each and every time she had tried to emerge from the falseness of yesterday, her previous existence would plunge her back. It was true that she had attempted to batter down the walls of her hopelessness, and although from time to time they were fewer and less wretchedly painful, she still suffered periods of deep fear. It was as though their shadow had the ability to over cloth her in its spite. The new world had delivered itself to her but the fire from the old world had disfigured her and held her in its yoke. Here in the woodlands, in this sanctuary of calm, she had composed special intentions for herself, but always without consulting her mirror. The new nest that she had weaved, away from her own enemy was good, but the thread had been carelessly woven. She could be so happy and, at times, she was, but was this really her journey's end? The sugared words that she had found here, were a rest from thought, but not a meaning; the meaning was still locked, awaiting rest, in the privacy of her lonely heart.

At times, she had begun to feel that the company of her tortured soul was an irreconcilable vulgarity. She was aware that it was not bitterness or malice, but there was still no lasting vision offered in a suppressed truth.

This beautiful hinterland created an embrace that she aspired to and craved, and she had fallen willingly and recklessly into it. These lovesome and unpretentious folk had given her a marble stage and allowed her to dip in the spotlight of their sympathetic world; was it all just a charity ball? Her fears were unfounded but they were fears nevertheless. They had made her sublime and her carnivorous heart had grasped and taken every honour in thankful greed. It had never been her intention or etiquette to take, and now she despised herself for it. She reasoned that her overindulgence and inherent behaviour had reached its boundary, and that she should disappear forever in the backwoods of these gentle folks' memories.

The sunlight was becoming old and yellow and she had become convinced that absence was her only weapon against a supreme arsenal of abounding hunger for this haven. She could never betray the warmth that they had bestowed upon her. She knew that she was a pretender, who wanted to respond, but could not.

Great, unbound sheaves of rain, washed across her soul. She shivered; her gooseflesh could hear the storm.

Wrapped in silence and frail like mom's delicate china, she stepped onto the outgoing bus.

THE SEQUEL

CHAPTER 1

S he headed north, feeling like she had been pushed or nudged by a hand of sure direction, without any real idea of where it would culminate. Sometimes only desperation can cut through any logic, and anything.

She thought of the old melodies that had no meaning, and the happy memories that did; but her attempts to find new solutions to old problems were a single game of solitaire; and when it ends, it would start up again. When she had fended away the old shadows, she was offered a safety net of sorts, and now in this new darkness she hungered for that light she had left behind; and dare not think what might replace it.

She liked the look of this town, it was 'Southern' looking and accommodated many white houses, fronted with tall, slim columns and poplar trees that shuffled around porch swings. In the space of that afternoon, she sat on a Sunday bench for a while and mused the coming of another day. She plodded through newspapers ads, and before long, she had rented a two-storey brick home, which was just one block West of the main thoroughfare. She particularly liked the bathroom, which contained a granite suite and oval window that gazed across a fenced yard of rumpled plants. The ceilings were cracked and the doorbell would buzz at odd times (due to a loose connection), but all in all, this house had a good ambiance about it.

When the last October sun had gone to its resting place beyond the lake, the interlude between evening and morning grew long, and the solitary chore of climbing the stairs, to maybe sleep, but not to think, became increasingly painful. The dark of days were disappearing, but the dark of nights and the truth that lay in wait at the top of the stairs were reoccurring. The inner wilderness of her soul was still planted with seeds unanswered.

Against the grain of reality, it was a rare day indeed when unexpectedly she refused to allow solitude to become her companion. Like an eight-grade girl who had just been invited to the spring hop, her head was high and her smile was on full. She had become weary of being the boss of her own company; she was needful of a neat, good-looking stranger to shoulder her life.

Excited by this brilliant and daring idea, she huddled into a warm coat and headed out toward 'Loony Lens'. It was as though all her wishes and surprises had been planned together in one package.

Len was the town's dog man: grooming, clipping and sleds outfitters, he was also the proprietor of the local pound. Although Len's handle implied that he was a half-wit, folks had fostered the title on account that his weird laugh was not dissimilar to the loon bird. He was very protective of his mutts and would not chuck them out to just anyone in a depersonalised fashion; he was very fastidious and fussy and always insisted upon the person having the dog of his choice. No doubt, this explained his oversized family!

She sat alone on a hastily constructed wooden bench among mops and pails, whilst Len disappeared to the end of a passage in order to find a suitable friend. She had an uncomfortable mixture of feelings that comprised of happiness, apprehension, and that peculiar weariness that comes with the relaxation of excitement.

The passage became suddenly alive with commotion, because there, straining on its leash, was the great North American consolation prize, – thirteen dollars worth of overweight love, – ready and willing to trample down the roses and take liberties on the front porch!

Len fixed his gaze upon her: 'You need to give him a name, I call him 'what have you', but he needs a proper name.' As though he was going through a resume, he continued, 'I could take you up one road and down another, but he's the boy for you, he'll see you right through tomorrow.'

She called him 'boy' for several days, but was obliged to put a feminine ending to his name, after 'he' suddenly produced a litter of pups; she had thought that his squatting down to pee was rather unusual!

They were halcyon days and 'active' nights. In the mornings, she would chop firewood, and at night she would sit with her feet on the stove and sing aloud to her espoused family; using just the raw ingredients of her voice, and their favourite chow. They were her heart's amulet, and had kindled a new courage within her.

Smiling broadly as she watched them tugging at the hem of her PJ's, she laughed: 'Hey, strays, I know where I am; do you?'

CHAPTER 2

The old house resounded with life, it was so different to the small echo that she had made on her own. Even when silence prevailed, it was good to be unafraid to share that silence.

Her limbs felt well oiled and she was spending the early am diligently exercising her rusty vacuum on its eager journey of house chores.

Her small audience were rolling and resting heavy lidded on the horizon of the lounge rug; seemingly pretending not to look at her, but innocently plotting a new path for their bowels and her brush.

It was brisk fall weather. The sky was undecided to reveal its ambivalence with snow or water, but in any event, it was the type of day when home is a cherished and abiding place to be. Her own patrician – like sereneness – surprised her, as though the old house had responded to her needs.

She ignored the buzz of the doorbell, as if it was some half-forgotten joke, but paused defensively to the entrapping sound of rapping upon the glass. Cautiously, she partly opened the door and positioned herself sideways in the aperture like a crab.

Awaiting tentatively on the porch were two rather business like people with a look that they had something to share with her; the woman was dressed with tweeds and her hair shingled up at the back; the man's impression was square from the jaw line to closely cropped hair.

She responsively presumed her visitors to be Jehovah's Witnesses or perhaps collecting for the town's Christmas fund. Regardless, it was an untimely moment for her to pursue questions from strangers.

Her pronunciation of 'good morning' was noticeable rippled, and so trying to be a little more forthright she added 'thank you, but not today, thank you.'

Almost interrupting her in mid-sentence the man responded 'morning ma'am' (he was studying her, comfortably but slightly spellbound) 'Aren't you—'...

'Yes', she interposingly replied.

'You were Hamilton's eminent chanteuse; saw you premiere in theatreland several years ago.'

Any star can be devoured by human adoration, sparkle by sparkle, and nesciently, he was breathing his way right through her. She could sense her patchwork quilt of confidence and hope splitting and tearing apart at its seams.

CHAPTER 3

During those bland autumn days, she had occupied her time with a new and sure passion; it was her possession and she had built a wall around it to keep trespassers out. This keepsake was a passion worth stopping for, and kept her from running away from the pry or demands, that no one should ever know or guess.

The solitude that brought her here had slowly exploited her plans, and made happy thoughts stretch and widen in her mind. Tardiness was no longer her surest enemy; it was simpler to move slowly, or not at all.

Although they had guessed her name, and she had at first allowed the disclosure to trouble her, she was just a frown away from being relieved. The thought that someone had written a speech particularly for her was consoling, and helped to navigate her away from the self-harm of murmuring misgivings and into rationality. Perhaps she had run fast, far and long enough, and finally reached the end of those dappled hovering shadows.

Speaking in a whisper, with her head tucked down in the narrow channel of her breasts she replied: 'Whatever I become was my first disguise'; immediately tossing her head back jubilantly she added, 'Don't be fidgeting on my porch; I serve good coffee, like some?' She had really demonstrated the cadence of her soft disembodied voice; an endorsement to her past professionalism!

They surrounded the gingham tablecloth and the enigmatic imprints began to lose trace of themselves as a new transformed rush of life sped through her arteries; it was as though her long walk home to confidence had finally arrived safely.

As if he was trying to memorize an unwritten script, the incomer anxiously made a meek adjustment to his necktie: 'I guess that everyone's getting heated about the Soviets and Cubans but we've got our own melancholic cub.' She kind of liked his quiescent attitude and quirky character; allowing him space to continue she tapped a pack of Camel and offered them out. 'Or would you prefer a stick of Beechnut?', she surmised, rummaging through her apron pocket.

The woman intercepted with moral support as though she knew this was going to be difficult for him (and afraid that he may get a kick in the pants!).

'I am Lynn, my brother Matt and I are joint principal at Willow Wood Montessori School.' She nodded, and was content to wait as her visitor briskly continued: 'your realtor is an acquaintance of ours, and we've put ourselves forward to ask your help.' Matt was still fumbling with a book of matches; Lynn gave him an endearing smile and began to succinctly relate: 'I imagine you will agree that every child should have music... any child who is deprived of music has been deprived of education.' Matt took a deep inhale and added: 'Sandra's only attribute to maturity is music; and that she smokes on the sly.'

Lynn overlapped his words: 'Music is Sandra's only ever true likelihood to finding her confidence.' As though he was having a conversation with himself Matt mumbled, 'She's an illegitimate kid... suffered a lot of social ostracism.' Lynn felt committed to add, 'She was taken in by the Greys, but they have a liquor problem and half the time are two potatoes short of a bushel.'

Matt had regained his posture: 'Sandra finds herself in music, it touches her; speaks directly to her. If we could chase her in your direction, perhaps your humming and honing would give her the beginning she's looking for.'

How often serendipity had played a part in her life and freed her from the uncertainty of applause.

The talk of ordinary people, and their need to be engaged in music, was always the basis of her inspiration; she evermore sidestepped the sham of artistes. Her passion for music never needed them; it was a need unto itself.

CHAPTER 4

S ometimes the wind of uncertainty can turn the pages, and people can lose a chapter because of hesitation; or the words that they need boil over onto a blank page of indifference; but she felt drawn toward this aura-movement and infinitesimal sipping from mutual love of plainsong.

Like a clock in a Dali painting, the fuzzy circumstances, of wept about time were melting away. Her existence felt divided in the knowing that the breathing in the shadows were not only her own.

Although she had never asked for an ally (or for anyone or anything) this was a prior action by others, and had not been instigated by herself. She had remained passive for too long and the answers had seldom come, but she felt heartened to be able to create a world for Sandra. It was a great undertaking and so little was required except of reciprocal love of music.

Harmony can gain access to the road of freedom, it can be a way of inching yourself from the dark side of the room to enlightenment. Perhaps her own pain would be extinguished in the ashes that lit it and she could give Sandra a recognition of the future, that would not be an entry into the world alone or without direction. It was a blank page and she would write the beginning with Sandra.

CHAPTER 5

She looked wrapped in magic, clothed in her famed velvety black dress, like a debutant at finishing school. She wanted to feel her worth, and with a hushed look of pride upon her face she gazed at her winsome family and pronounced 'What ya think?' Rehearsal was always an important facet, but in her way of coming round, she felt it necessary to audition herself as well.

She practiced long and hard that day and as the light began to dissolve through the lacy white drapes, she had travelled back across the lyrical nakedness of time, to the songs and styles that used to be her trademark; she had also mastered a whole pack of smokes and a carafe of wine!

Intermittently her menagerie had given accompaniment; it was a remarkable duet by a virtuoso and supporters but added nothing to the lessons!

From time to time, she would wave her flounced sleeves at them, like a scarecrow in the wind in an effort to subdue the caterwaul; and for several moments, they would stare back and salivate abundantly like Pavlov's dog; their repertoire was impatiently endless.

When Sandra was scheduled in to meet her for supper on Saturday, she prepared a dream of delectable goodies; she was a sinful cook, it had to be rich, sweet and easy: like Rocky Road Pie (with extra chocolate bars) and oatmeal Rocks (with extra walnuts and raisins). It was a desire to please, combined with a sugary cunning promise of a script to follow.

CHAPTER 6

Her misgivings began to surface as Saturday approached. She wanted to plead a severe cold, but every material aspect of planning was in place and there was really nothing left to do except to go ahead with the event.

The last several hours of expectations and waiting were devouring her composure; she kept busying with silly inconsequential antidotes to assure herself that everything was perfect; it was as though she was expecting a whole regiment of students to suddenly come clanking into her drawing room. For a rare period in her career she need not have worried, for when time finally uncoiled, the euphoria of Sandra rapping the door, made her feel discovered and whole again.

Their smiles connected effusively and she felt drawn to her immediately; her freckled expression and dark brown bangs emphasized a jaunty face with no trace of coyness.

She was going through that roly-poly puberty stage and looked more content to eat cheesecake, rather than pose for it; and yet the haze of wonder in her freshness was a promise of tomorrow that does not look like today.

Followed by a tiny giggle, she dissected a rainbow coloured pen from a studious bunch of coloured pencils that were sticking out of her breast pocket like porcupine quills and inquired, 'May I have permission for your autograph, ma'am?' The words had quite unexpectedly tumbled toward her so naturally that for the first time in many years she had enjoyed the question; it seemed like an eventful compromise. She discretely replied, 'I am flattered you have asked, but please understand my name is not an explanation of me.'

They sat comfortably by the wood burner and yarned together in the zaniest manner; as though Sandra had gained maturity and her tutor had returned to adolescence – and somewhere in between they met. Sandra was the shape of those ideals that had shrunk so strangely within her life; she was Kennedy's promise and Piaf's voice; in spite of its resonance through missing front teeth!

The long mirror that she had meticulously rehearsed her reflection in was reproducing its critical importance of detail to them both.

As the evening neared its voyage end, she gazed fondly at Sandra and surmised, 'We have written many new paragraphs this evening through happy dialogue; our dialogue has been our music; with any good song you can just recite it and it still becomes music.' Unhurried, she added, 'Tell me your stories in your chansons and we will put music to them. You will find the starting of a new story easier than the ending. When the ending becomes hard, don't let your characters take command. If people assume that you desire glory or pelf, you will become a windup toy. If you "want" you will be cheated by them and yourself. Be confident in your own ability and it will be them that 'want' and you who dictate.'

CHAPTER 7

The contented autumn weeks were briskly whirling by. It seemed that, at last, her picture of life was steadily growing in stature and colour. The bleak headlines and images of mushroom clouds and declaration of intent, that foreshadowed the insufferable outside world, were hollow specks of insignificance in her new and joyous world.

Matt would shuffle back and forth with Sandra; the making of each day was pristine and fresh with excitement and expectation.

It was late November; heavy sleety rain was emptying from the upside down sky like huge grey sponges, and leaves were flying dazed in the wind. Almost buried in the harshness of the night, Matt's chafed wood-sided station wagon, laboured slowly and laboriously to a halt in her driveway, to chaperon Sandra home. Wiping the wet moonlight from his temple, he stumbled up the porch steps toward the hospitable light dancing in the doorway. 'All in all, this fall's weather has been hard,' he tiredly remarked. 'Been imagining your coffee all the way over here.'

Sandra was watching him interestedly, as though she was exhaustively evaluating his every move. 'It's all right, ma'am', she surmised, 'he's only nervous; got a lot of things to do; a lot on his mind; don't you, sir?' Without pausing, and with her eyes shining eagerly, she hastily continued, 'May I have a chocolate shake, ma'am; with three full scoops... you make a mean shake.'

Matt had picked out his comb and was running it idly through his short wet hair; there was a snow-white starchiness about him, and although his words came like the wind dragging small dirigibles through the pines, there was undoubtedly something amusing gained from them. 'Twentieth century folk in Indian Lodges, that's what we are', he agitatedly remarked, 'no smarter than a skeena salmon.' She craned her neck away from her busyness in the kitchen and touched him fondly with her eyes, 'Your words have a distinctive familiar echo; my Dad's outlook was that even if we stood on tiptoe, we still could not grasp the future.'

Sandra was helping her to prepare some corn chowder for Matt, and as she handed her the skillet, she put her innocent face close to her cheek and in a rich comforting and knowing voice whispered, 'Small boys need encouragement, the trains in their minds will only take them so far, ma'am.'

She did like Matt, and it was true that an endearing light mist had formed a question mark between them; but she was still navigating between her instinct and her rationality; it seemed like an impasse situation.

On the other hand, he seemed unable to portray his feelings toward which his senses propelled him; perhaps because her very existence was a sign of her passive remoteness that he wanted to respect and observe.

Although there were occasions when the rooster of time would awaken their capability of uttering a string of words; and the cross fire of their glances would quietly reach their captive hearts; there was still a timorous uneasiness. If the dream was a tricked reality of doubt, why was there forever hope and a glowing shiver?

She still walked alone in the past tense, and was tiring of being stained with loneliness; and weary of the empty side of slumber, where the sun never sets and where insomnia keeps watch.

CHAPTER 8

The moon was brightly cleaving the layers of milky snow with such colourless diamante that it almost hurt the eyes. Pitilessly, the wind was rising to meet the evening and slowly blowing away the drowsy fog that had been hanging in the pines and shrouding the neighbourhood all day.

She combed ponderously through her russet hair and gazed passed her iced bedroom window glass at the gaunt trees; she was deep in thought and her eyes were somewhere else. As though the loosened hair had removed all hesitation, she laid down the bone-handle comb and hurried fleetingly down the stairs; her face looked saddened, as if she had been locked up and forgotten about.

Sandra was sitting by the hearth, brushing and chatting with the dogs in childish utopia and delighting herself as the fire eat through its uninterrupted meal of rank hairs.

She stepped determinedly out into the black mouth of the night and hastily made her way through the fog that was still clinging to the intersection. Stepping across the boughs and dead tree trunks, she weaved steadily along the cold south shore of the lake. The still black water lay beckoning in obscene silence; coaxing like a cemetery of want that could dismember and unfreeze a person's logic.

Her heart was beating like a million hammers on stone; she remembered everything not worth the brutal remembering; and how she had negated her helter-skelter life and traded it for the bitter freedom of abandoned worthlessness to alleviate a dignity not worth dignifying.

When Matt arrived at the house, Sandra was sat at the typewriter with tinsel in her hair and a rosy Christmas apple in her hand. As though she was having a private conversation with herself, she preambled: 'I'm writing a SONG OF MYSELF; not as lengthy as Walt Whitman's, of course', she proclaimed stridently. 'I wish that I could whistle a tune to it.'

Her pretty conversation was dissolving incoherently in his head: a table, a chair, a desk, the festive lights and decorations; the place was banal and empty without her. Trying to steer away from the veil of foreboding that was engulfing him, he apprehensively asked 'It's late, where has she wandered?' Sandra looked at him petulantly and replied, 'Oh, to the lake.'

In an uproar of silence, he ran outside, as if his legs were treading on air and his heart was filled with the agitation of nettles. He felt his world bending over in the shame that he did not go beyond the words he now needed to tell her.

It was she, who had given him an embroidered plateau of meaning and purpose, and it was she who had stolen into his night's slumber and implanted dreams that reached out for him to aspire to. It was she, his nightingale of bequeathed destiny, who had flown from his seemingly indifferent recognition; now the realization lay embedded in the encumbered and tortured bitterness of his soul.

The moon had become a sickle, a golden scythe of doom. The first stars were anxiously hungering for attention but were obscured by his confused frosted breath.

It was as though the bracken he was running through had finally ripped away and defoliated his inherent constraints and he had awoken in a clearing of vision.

Through the ghostly frosted crystal of mist, he glimpsed her frail luminous outline, fine etched in the limpid moonlight.

It was as though she had suddenly emerged from some subterranean passage, like a star dancing magically bright upon the snow. As she ventured toward him, he could detect her ominous heavy breathing and a conspiring rustling sound. He stood mortified for a moment, an absolute moment... until, there concealed and unveiled behind an innocent bunch of mistletoe was a beautiful broad smile, with a jaunty slant of a lit cigarette.

She had finally informed her thankless life of nothing deeper, more simple, or greater than a heart that wanted to start afresh. He watched the mist blowing against her face and arms; an identical moment had found them both. 'I've brought some encouragement,' she said chuckling; her voice swarmed like a gentle breeze all around him. He gazed at her endearingly and uttered, 'Do you know what time it is?' She lifted his arm and glanced at his watch. 'It's five after midnight and twenty seconds.' As though he had acquired some great perception, he replied, 'It's Christmas!' She looked straight at him and wholeheartedly replied, 'Merry Christmas, Matt!' Disburdened, he sighed, 'Merry Christmas, Kim!'

CHAPTER 9

Like a peacock spreads its fan, Matt began building an alter for her; a grotesque creation of prefabricated adversity. He scheduled her to conduct a brief interview with the Daily Student Newspaper and soon every direction became an interplay of questions and autographs from an intrusive audience; it was a recurrent theme of her life and had all became rather familiar.

Matt would say its ok; but alone it was far from it; his divided loyalties were difficult to deal with, and became a concussion that gouged her mind and wrenched her sobbing heart. He threw her crumbs of his complex love that left her starving; it was as though she could hear his zealous kisses at the door but there was no unity when he came in. He would drool over her and the intensity in his steel blue eyes would shine, but there seemed to be a stone in his heart that would sink beneath all his forsaken wisdom.

He introduced her to a conflicted insipid relationship with the town's strange brotherhood of artsy types and although the relationship was not completely without affection (she felt there was some level of empathy) it was complicated and more than she had bargained for. She was not yearning for acceptance. She was seeking conceptual understanding.

They undressed her vision and saluted her with an interpretation of academic garbage that was full of cultural clichés and self-glorifying stereotypes of the sketchy artist they presumed her to be. It was as though they had this adolescent fantasy about her, and it was not as she wanted to be perceived, as a person or an artist. Beneath their unwashed suits and dirty nylons was a pretentious and pompous ritzy life style of opinions that they assumed was serious art and politics.

Their social statements on how to govern Canada and make the French talk English, was as comic as it was absurd; they were a personification of the problem and cartoons of the truth.

There was so much personal stuff going on and they expected her to be nourished by this modern love and all that it offered. Their addiction was no more than a creative breakdown. It was sending her to destruction, she was afraid, insecure; had all her life been a preface to this?

Matt was oblivious that the atmosphere of torture was a conspiracy against his misappropriate love and that their detached voices were mutilating her; it was as though his mind was eclipsed and overawed by his own fulfilment.

She had become self-protective of her dutiful appeal and sometimes felt like strangling the telephone as it danced summoning before her; or strangling 'them' when they would reward her with a kiss; communication style!

The déjà vu memories sent a chill through her and in the hollow of the night she could still detect their voices screaming in her cold and numb world. Her life had become so crowded, but she was so alone.

It was like some big movie premier and when the show was over, she had consulted the mirrors in the lobby many times before on her way out.

CHAPTER 10

When she was a kid, she had started to write a poem dedicated to Dorothy Gale. She had stopped for the same reason that she had started it in the first place, and could never bring it to a satisfactory conclusion. She wanted desperately to conjure the colours of that somewhere, somewhere rainbow, but even with the most touching words spread all over the page, she found it impossible; and now a labyrinth of manic, hard to recognize, frozen and unwritten words smouldered to be heard; still leading somewhere, anywhere, nowhere. Like Dorothy, she too was living in a land not drawn on any map, and the asphalt road lay ahead like a transparent canvas; it promised and demanded, like ice cream odours, and raced toward her fast and seductive.

The forbidding landscape was innocently waiting and abiding for her to un-nail her secret luggage of error and truth.

She sat at the chiffonier and began to meticulously remove the paint from her face, like it was the ashes of the day, and thought of Matt. She felt a certain kind of fragmented sympathy for him: he was separated from his sight, his voice, (she could still hear him command her to be happy) his heart and dead eyes. He was like some vast waste, which threatened never to leave her. She had a mountain of recriminations imposed upon herself, without his contributions as well.

Maybe she had become more resilient, because there were no longer floods of tears in her eyes; just the debris of broken dreams in her heart and unseen cries that tried to shelter her body from the open wounds. He had given her an unfathomable prepacked intellect of slaughtered half-frozen words, and now she balanced upon the knives edge of sick non-existence and longed for the beautiful precipice.

She peered intently at the hostile sky, it seemed that even God had become benumbed at the snow of sorrow that had settled over everything; there was enough for the whole winter, and another winter. Although she had stopped searching for reasons, she had never been disloyal to her principles and refused to allow herself to be the conquered and them the conquerors. She had reached that point of sorrow where gigantic waves of orgasm can intervene, and fend off the cruel caress of mockery; her sad mask still knew how to smile... at her own pain.

Her illusion, her poem: snowed under by nicotine and sleeping pills; she stepped outside and felt the snowflakes settle on her head like a halo. For her, there was always a veil of light that separates art from life, and the imperishable images of chimeras and wizened witches would have to wait for an answer, because she could still answer for herself.

CHAPTER 11

Time lagged along, and she no longer cared if she heard or did not hear. As the chorus of ragged voices grew, so did her silence.

It was not that she had lost her power of choice, on the contrary, she had indeed found an answer to the question of what was left; and the remains were her heirloom of being somewhere. The house no longer winced or resounded its demons when silence prevailed and sleep refused to come; it was as though her brain had become a basement that was emptier than thought. The atmosphere of torturous reality had pretty much become a self- fulfilling prophecy and a cancerous comfort that led and paralleled her every move.

She had recently taken to watching the old late-night movies on channel 7; it was a happy repression of sorts. She cogitated on how strange it was that the heroes never change: Bogart still wears his trench coat; Dooley Wilson still plays 'as time goes by.'

Although the movie had kept her up way past her bedtime; and she had watched it many times before; she nevertheless still revelled in each captivating word, and was glad they kept repeating it. She had never really understood the reason why Bogie had jilted Bergman in Paris; was that really necessary? Maybe it was a scrambled recompense, a way of sacrificing the present for the future.

She remembered watching it for the first time with some beau's pitiful dandruff; they had arrived late, just as the movie was exacting its climax. She recalled stumbling through shoes in the darkness in order to find a seat; and how the popcorn was so sticky, and she could not find a Kleenex.

Time had turned away, reel by reel, and although there was always an anonymous arm to take at the exit, there was still no hero waiting for her at an unexpected rendezvous in destiny. Each journey was a cheap and meandering release from concealed reality.

February was a cheerless month, an impatient month, that wanted to move on and yet was too cumbersome to do so. Its incumbent stalagmites hung uncompromising like fruit bats in an ancient portcullis, straight, uniformed and defiant, from the frozen soffits, each uttering the undaunted courage of winter's refrain.

She gingerly stepped out onto the porch to shake the breakfast crumbs out into the afterglow of evening and smiled with amusement at the early birds picking and quarrelling under the eves, where the titbits and spiders had planted themselves. Retreating back into the warmth quickly, she showered and slipped into a smart black dress; the product of a rather expensive Toronto shop.

Sandra had stayed over for several days, on account of the weather and such, and was sitting with her legs swung over a wide armed chair reading intently. 'What are you reading?' she asked. 'Oh, just a childish fairy tale, I like to read them once in a while,' she soberly replied. She reached out and put her fingertips against Sandra's cheek. Sandra kept her nose in the book and extended an affectionate hand to hold hers.

She sat for a few moments staring and contemplating the old clock on the wall dragging time by, as if there was a family pageant scheduled and the expectancy was too much to wait for. Hastily stubbing out her first smoke, as though it had become an obstacle, she elated. 'We've got pints of gumption haven't we?' Sure that she had Sandra's attention she added swiftly, 'Pray like a Catholic, honey, today we're going to find you a homecoming.'

CHAPTER 12

She had recently purchased a vintage Chevy from a guy who could talk the ears of a moose. She started the motor running for the heater's sake, and they both spluttered into cough laughing at the stink of gasoline. With Sandra flopped comfortably across the bench seat, and after considerable finagling with the choke, they set off to Sandra's house.

She still possessed the skill of resourcefulness, and by the time they arrived, she had assumed a commanding moral sense of determination: to get Sandra out of her hapless knot; in all its forms.

No one had ever developed any plan for Sandra, she had spent too much of her life being nudged from orphanage to so-called temporary care, and back. All they had ever offered her was an address with an empty room. It was all just a trade-off of concessions: She complicated peoples' lives, and they felt obliged to complicate hers.

It was unfortunately true that the Greys did have a liquor problem, although it did not appear to present a problem to them. Their gittin' bitched was a filamentary engaging combination of their quirky delirious humour and character. Their demeanour in many respects was quite endearing; though slightly giddy.

Mr Grey welcomed them in, set up several bottles of cheap wine and mumbled, 'We're not degenerates, but no wine, no magic'; he then began to run through a resume of his tattoos.

When eventually they had reached the boundary where even lost souls can penetrate, the conversation began to formulate into long platitudes of reminiscence. She liked these people, even the fact that they were wearing galoshes around the house, had a kind of simplistic nicety.

She waited patiently, and when eventually it seemed appropriate, she broached the agenda she had been leading toward.

He gripped her hand, shook it profusely and thanked her. It was as though he was appeased to have made a miraculous bond with an angel that was not a dishonourable compromise of his so-called drowsy life. If indeed, behind everyone an angel does keep watch, then truly Mr Grey had made a bond with an angel; in any event, it was a paradoxical coupling.

They loaded Sandra's charitable belongings in the trunk and drove to River Heights: a slightly elevated point that panorama's over the old and new parts of town. It was a popular venue for courting couples during evening hours, and a beautiful vantage point: the weather was clear and crisp, and you could see the belfry of the school, the church spires and the winding blue road of the river that separated the old from the new. Thin worms of smoke came from the old houses on the South shore, whilst on the North shore the new houses enjoyed all-round oil heating.

Sandra had taken over the rear seating and had foraged some Hershey bars from the picnic tray. She was sitting like a mannequin in a store window: upright, expectant and knowingly inquisitive. She leaned across the seat and began to speak to Sandra in a small whisper, as if she had just plotted a surprise concert. 'Hey, you,' Sandra shouted and added affectionately, 'My singer of pathos used her talent today'. Sandra began to recite the Canadian, American and Russian joke: She looked at Sandra indirectly through the driver mirror and asked, 'Well, would you care to share the impoverished show of my life?' There was a silence of gaiety as Sandra meticulously licked the tip of her well-sharpened pencil and began to write:

1. Wakes-up too damn early and has a Camel for breakfast.
2. Gossips endlessly to herself.
3. In the habit of hiding her cigarettes.

4. Cooks well But does she eat?
5. Speaks like she's writing on air.
6. Paints her face like a park bench.
7. Keeps a great four-poster empty nuptial bed.

Sandra surveyed each comment, paused, considered them briefly, and began ticking each item. Finally, she signed the document with the chutzpah of a downtown lawyer, and had written underneath in bold capitals: '**YES!**'

'Sounds like a pretty slick impoverished show to me,' she added cheekily.

Her small gifted hand had just carved a miracle for them both.

She felt a tear welling-up; a gigantic one; flooding the world, just as light floods into a new pristine summer morning.

CHAPTER 13

A light feathery silence of snowflakes had settled and was complimenting the winter's worth of grimy snow mounds like a pristine made-up bed. In the second week of March, the worn-out winter was rapidly succumbing to the fervent embraces of another defiant season.

She lazed in the rocking chair, resting her head, luxuriating and untangling the day's events in her mind; a rapping at the door unexpectedly intruded upon her thoughts. Sandra had been sitting among a flighty disarrangement of bewildered jigsaw pieces, with her canine audience remonstrating, as she pigged-out on chocolate cookies; but hearkening to the rapping she immediately brushed the cookie crumbs from her skirt, and in a bustle of barks and bounds, they hotfooted to the door. She rose lazily from the rocker (it was evident that her accomplices had matters under control) and tried to speculate on why someone was prompted to visit at this late hour?

Sandra had already opened the front door, delivered a cheery 'hi', but had not welcomed the visitor in.

A stylish woman shuffled in the cold, with rather an uncomfortable half- smile; she was dressed in an expensive well-made cony fur, her high-collared coat was touching her chin, and her hands were protected in a fur-muff.

'We're not inhospitable, ma'am, please come inside,' Sandra quipped.

The woman held out a compensating limpish hand, 'Glad to finally meet you, my name is Evelyn Levine, I represent Belmont Levine Associates; how do you do.'

She pulled a chair out for the woman, patted the cushion; and as if diverting from the matter in hand; complimented 'Your white Lincoln looks magnificent.' Pausing briefly and summoning her artistic courage, she added, 'Well, I am at your service, but I'm not sure how I can possibly help you.'

Feeling that her embellished smile was now inappropriate the woman took a deep breath, beckoned her saddest voice and apprehensively plunged in, 'Your father died of diphtheria... several months ago... we had difficulty in locating you.' Her voice yielded several moments and she continued, 'he gave us power of attorney... his Will is very specific, all his wishes involved the protection of you.'

She looked strangely unmoved, she felt that she had long since left him behind; although she had always missed him, she couldn't even hear his voice any longer, only imagine him.

It was true, she had grieved for him for years, but now it was as though all the grieving had already been endured and admonished. She had nursed a storefront of dreams, they were valuable returning dreams, ingrained and waiting patiently for him; for the day when he would be her audience, and she could sing in defiance from the bottom of her belly, with all the air she had.

Sandra interceded her thoughts. 'I can hear your mind whining, no one is guilty, ma'am.'

'Thank you, honey,' she replied in a matter of fact way. She raised the cup and finished the coffee dregs, and with a waving hand in a gesture of anxiety, hastened the woman to continue.

'Although he bequeathed you some real estate over on Lake Erie, it's really his letter that prompted my visit.' The woman took a document from her briefcase and began to succinctly relate:

My Krysia,

When your mother passed away during the winter of '52, her early death left me bitter, I felt it was a treachery that could not be defined. Your mother and I wanted beyond all want for you, we wished beyond all reason for you, and her passing dictated my future, and yours. Missing her became a paralysis, and when the air grew too heavy to breath, I realised I could no longer protect my paper child. It was as though we had always shared the same fears for you and I was inadequate and unable to carry the burden of responsibility alone. When I bundled you off to boarding school, I hoped your youth would cushion you. I am so sorry I did not see your graduation.

Please forgive my silence and regrets; although I muddled past you and feared returning, your needs were always known to me; only in the safety of these belated words can I finally reach out and speak.

When she slipped, so had her dreams, but he had always been her constant audience, his applause was an intense and deafening love, ever faithful and everlasting. Her unsung song had been heard, and now she had listened to his. Their dreams were never oblivious, merely locked away, safe, waiting for reunion. Safe and secure, in his soul, in his heart, and in the ground of their eternity.

The woman thanked them and left.

Playing hopscotch with Sandra, using the carpet squares that were two feet bigger, she was possessed with a strange new relish. Eventually they retired to bed.

She lay between the frigid bed sheets and watched the dark images smouldering across the cracked bedroom ceiling; even now, unprepared, she remembered:

Clip-clopping along beside him that confusing, grotesque day, as he accompanied her to the boarding school.

It was a beautiful late afternoon, and the sun was leaving bands of colour across the snow. She still retained the horrid spectre of the brooding school towers; they were a menacing impression to haunt the edges of any child's mind. She recollected how her cotton skirt had brushed against some bare rosebushes, being caught here and there on the thorns; and how she had wanted to pull the simpering bows off the

Principal's ostentatious dress. She remembered gripping his hand relentlessly tight, like a small child crossing a busy city thoroughfare for the first time; harnessed to his body, holding on... and the wrench of letting go. She remembered feeling the residue of bewilderment as she descended the stairs, carrying her small cardboard suitcase and being escorted to her procrustean bed in the dormitory of rag-dolls. She remembered the gush longing in her body to run home when they began to mercilessly shave her hair short.

The school was a quagmire of crass elitism that was adverse to her slight, soft Polish inflection, and the fact that she had the impoverished appearance of a twelve-year-old. She remembered all the unanswered letters; it had all been his act, and now it was an absolute; complete and entire; but she still remembered.

Her throat restrained the sobs; they were controlled and quiet. The room grew greyer, her thoughts decimated, and she slept.

CHAPTER 14

S he sat in the window, enclave shaping her fingernails and idly watching a flock of swans spread out into the morning, ruffling the daybreak and the water.

She reflected upon the milestone of the previous evening: when that solitude of reflection is the solitude of loving and sharing the same fears, there are tears without eyes, and guilt can even dapple the sweet-scented wind of a born new day.

The snow was disappearing fast and the long day ahead looked uninspiring and transparent; the type of day when the only bedrock of comfort is to count every eccentric blessing and total them with frayed optimism. She began to deliberate upon the new positive merits of her existence, she thought about Sandra, such a tiny disturbance, and yet an inescapable treasure, a pool of clear water in which she mirrored herself. Like complementary colours they had heightened and intensified each other's lives, and now definitively mixed, they had become brighter, confident and more vibrant. Their higgledy-piggledy lives were a curious oxymoron to find peace, but like snowdrops in pre-spring, it was an atonement of sorts.

Unexpectedly, the patterns in her mind abruptly burst into a storm of petals; she began to feel in a state of such a high brilliance, and bore little resemblance to the person who had moments before been staring lifelessly through the windowpane. Her mind was overtaking itself as she hastily tapped upon Sandra's bedroom door in expectation; with new heedful plans flooding her thoughts.

Sandra dampened her glow somewhat, with a quick-fire, hotchpotch reply, 'Come-in, come-in, I'm watching Lucy; don't talk, come-in.' She sat cross-legged on the soft quilt observing Sandra (as though it would somehow precipitate the credits or station identification!). Finally she painfully interrupted 'Be sweet, honey; I've a surprise for you.'

Sandra took her eyes away from the screen and looked straight at her with tightened lips, in a weak mockery of anger, and sniggered, 'As long as you are not kneeling in tears again, I want to know, right now.'

She felt that she was ready for this decision, it had been a long process, an eternity of sorrow, happening in clumsy interrogating stages, but for her conscience and sanity, this would become her confession; a renunciation of the past; a biography, where mystery and pain no longer can survive. It was true, she still felt like running; like deserting from this privilege, which had tempted her; but nevertheless, her mouth and heart were now so eager to go beyond the boundaries of lingering resignation.

Slowly, like she was over concerned, with unimportant details she began her pictorial to Sandra: 'The city is a strange place honey, each day everything seems to carry on as it did the day before, only the people threading their way through the crowds change. It's so full of colours, smells and sounds you could never imagine. There are Victorian mansions, restaurants with buckets full of delicious victuals of every possible variety. There are streetcars and cabs by the dozen and... River Creek Shopping Centre. Sooo, you pack, I'll escort the mutts to Len's, for their vacation, and then we're off on our excursion.'

Sandra bounced off the bed like an acrobat on a trampoline, almost overbalancing in her eagerness, but stopped short with concern: 'You quite sure that you want to do this, ma'am? The city also hurt you so bad.' She fixed a tender look on Sandra and replied, 'Not the city, honey, just the briar of gullibility.' In her mind she added 'and the second, when you can't start over again.'

CHAPTER 15

Sometimes the calendar is less victorious than the legend, and sometimes a mistake is fondly forgotten by a generation of new buds who revere the legend. She had never been a cliché star, she was purely the tainted mistress of this city, more than even she had ever thought possible. The sidewalks beckoned her; still wrapped in cobwebs and buried beneath a golden haze of dust, she was astonished how eyes still followed her in Dominion Square. Several anonymous hands reached out to welcome her and Sandra had even offered an elderly well-wisher a handkerchief, who cried 'I prayed for your soul, Kim.'

Exhausted from the hectic days shopping spree, they caved-in on a bench in Nathan Park. It was around 5pm and the early commuters were hustling and bustling past.

A chauffeur driven Rolls Royce pulled discretely up and a voice rang out: 'Kim and Sandra, the notorious couple. I would never have believed that I could miss you so much, Kim. Get in.'

His name was Jacques Leyrac; he was a suave, elegant-looking man of mature years. She'd always had a marvellous rapport with him. He was the one and the only impresario, who had guarded her name from the assassins. In the early days of her career, he had disciplined her and encouraged her; Jacques had always treated her like the ultimate Queen. He taught her the truth; and that bits and pieces of technique do not attract themselves to a single intelligible person. Jacques would laboriously prepare her repertoire of arias, choosing them and discussing them with her. But as she climbed the ladder of recognition, she betrayed him; looking for new deals. new ugly and manipulative deals, that made her become unsalable.

He looked at her seriously, 'When you left. this city lost its heart, Kim, your voice could tame kings and clowns; but not the madmen. hey?' She looked pensively into her lap, 'It stopped whispering words of love to me, Jacque.'

He puffed on his cigar ostentatiously. 'I know how it became an unremitting struggle for you, I guess when they couldn't win. they just cut you down. The same thing happened to Dietrich: scientific street fighting they call it.'

Jacques smiled at her compassionately, 'You should have come back to me, Kim.' She reached out, squeezed his knee fondly, and laughed 'I couldn't afford you, Jacque'

His attention turned to Sandra, 'Now Sandra, she's really a new candidate for my affections.' Sandra pulled a grimace and sank well back in her seat. 'It's ok sweetie pie, we'll just keep it platonic for now', he chuckled. She smiled at Sandra's awkwardness, 'It's totally all right, honey, he's homosexual.' Sandra beamed and replied, 'Cool, I never met one of those before.'

Jacque summoned his serious voice again. 'Kim, I'm plotting a new, great concert; you're a phenomenon, both as a person and as an artiste; I want you to begin it for me... and end it for you. One last performance, Kim, you need it: to forgive yourself and your fans will do likewise.' 'They poisoned my air with their gratified desires, Jacque; just erase my name from your mind', she replied sternly. He put his warm arm around her shoulders, and subdued, she freely rested her head upon his chest. 'You owe me, kid' he whispered. 'If your alter-ego agrees and Sandra approves, we'll call it a deal, ok?' 'Am I entering hell or heaven, Jacque?' she replied softly; but she knew she had captured that second in time when the opportunity to begin over was delivered, when music was nearer to peace than silence.

This was her ultimate chance, an exercise of freedom. defiance against the tyrants of the past, a resume of her life expressed by confrontation. They would arrive for her confession, and she would surrender it. There were many occasions when she would spend hours in front of the mirror, rehearsing and trying out new gestures. This time she did not need impressive gestures, all of her life had been a rehearsal for this moment. This time it was a matter of instinct and pure communication from the depths of her lonely heart to every individual soul mate in the audience.

CHAPTER 16

Her Finale

She stood in the wings, among the tinfoil and stars, waiting for the introduction. 'Don't let me do it alone, Sandra, be right here', she whispered in a faint voice. Her face was ashen as the moment suddenly came to life, and she walked out into centre stage; the curtain was hung in the middle to make the stage look smaller, but even so she looked frail and lost.

The lights dimmed and the spotlight burst upon her in unity; she stood motionless, hiding behind her bold dark spectacles and watching the blue haze of tobacco smoke as it rose, twirled and fell. As though she has just emerged from some primeval darkness, there was a deafening silence; the entire auditorium seemed to have become tongue-tied in a deadlock of disbelief.

With the virtuality of some divine intervention, the whole theatre suddenly lit up in a roaring frenzy like a cathedral on fire, but these were not sacrificial flames; she was once again Canada's Babylonian Queen, their courtesan, and they were on their feet to salute her, like a pack of respectful howling wolves under a sky of love. Tears flowed, the walls shook and the floor reverberated in welcome; and then, swift and utter silence.

There was an abnormal intrinsic quality to her performance. She had extended the range of her voice, breathing and conveying emotion to a pitch close to mania itself. Never like this had any audience understood and identified with another person's pain. Her lungs battered the air with such monumental sincerity; she sang in a total delirium of communication with every possible and powerful instinct available to her; it was the most stimulating and emotionally draining reciprocal union of compassion and spirit. Her voice was the embodiment of speech and music and perpetual suffering; a self-transformation of language; the singer's restless search for herself, and the uniqueness of her being.

The performance concluded and Sandra frantically ran across stage to hold her. Her arms collapsed around Sandra like a weeping angel. The applause thundered and rippled through the mosaic terraces and marble halls, gushing in torrents of adulation.

As the audience brayed 'encore', the world was oblivious as two diminutive figures in head-scarves hurried across Nathan Park and out into the consuming night. 'My ears are still throbbing, ma'am,' said a small voice.

When Jacque arrived at her dressing room, he was slightly bemused to find her gone, but smiled knowingly at the note written in pale lipstick across the mirror: – 'I love you Jacque, gone to check out Lake Erie.'

She had required the sureness of the shadows to make her complete; and the certainty of the shadows for her swan song; and now; the knowing that the necessity of that March evening would never repeat itself again.

LIMBERLOST INTERNALIZED

INTERNALIZED CHAPTER 1

S ometimes it seems that the more unpredictable an aversive event is, the less negative it can actually turn out to be; and so it came about that conclusive March evening. Eventually all the desolate and solitary paths that had been leading back to her, had unobtrusively led her back to the real linchpin of her own dilemma and spirit. When the past had called its indictment she was only able to finally see ahead because each epoch of time was beginning to glance backwards at her. Indeed, at first she had been relentlessly shoved and pushed so far in one direction, that it almost became the accepted tendency not to gravitate toward the roll of coming in any type of opposite direction; no matter how attractive or normalised an idea it evoked.

Her one hour of beautiful madness and indescribable joy. Her mind and her music were enshrined together, they had always been so much more than just an egocentric eye. They were her innate flame that wounds and flings itself about with ever empowered abandon; the very essence of noble elixir; a life so audience concerted that it is impossible to ever be given or taken in small uncomplicated sips.

Like a love dismembered doll who had been suffocated and buried in quilted sleep, her resurrected body could intuitively still feel the old affections and afflictions. It was as though 'total' misery had cried 'wait' and cautiously her life was rising again, like thankful little bruises.

INTERNALIZED CHAPTER 2

T hey journeyed contentedly toward Erie, into and through a hinterland of enveloped twilight and mystic beauty that forever ebbs on the fervent grandeur of dreams. A secret yesterday world where empathetic whispers can really permit the past to revisit and swirl caringly and responsively like a gramophone of time. At an unspecified moment its overtone may insist upon bringing a brand new beginning to the present, or at the very least, a new ending to the past.

Although modernism was slowly finding Canada, it was generally navigatedly drawn towards the largest centres, like Montreal and Toronto. Steering away from the fretting cold jungle of corporate contemporary Canada and its confused visions, another seemingly unimpeachable and very credible arcadian world was still enduring in its own unfeigned enclaves; and was proud of such.

INTERNALIZED CHAPTER 3

S low and majestically, like a parodied damask hearse that had
strayed from a satirical cortege, the white walls and eldorado fins
cavalcaded through the solitary wolf grey eventide.

Sandra was putting her own peculiar language to patriotism in a
kind of frisky (but heartfelt) manner: 'Eau Canada, Gloria's unfree!
Wheeze tendon guard, wheeze tendon guard 'fore thee. Eau Canada,
wheeze tendon guard 'fore thee!'

'This is a cool excursion at 37 mph,' said a tired voice in the rear
seat, rolling her eyes at the speedometer. 'Do they have some nice kids
where we're goin' ma-am?' she added buoyantly. Kim glanced
casually through her glazed day dream and into the brown tinted rear
view mirror. 'All roads have a slight scent of loneliness after sundown,
don't you agree honey?'

The worn transmission droned an accompaniment to a timely
metallic melody. She had always adored the bleating of lonely
sentimental ballads and enjoyed humming along to the refrain; eyes
smudged and drenching each lyric with her inwrought perception.

The greater the distance behind them grew, the more she became in
control of her time and space; even the gathering of her tears were a
somewhat intentional pleasure.

Her renewed and newly acquired freedom had given her and
revealed an almost noble and indolent air of calmness and relaxed
softness. She felt as pure as an angel and yet maybe deceived,
misplaced and fickle; as true love is to capture and to keep.

INTERNALIZED CHAPTER 4

By the time they arrived at Homestead Hill, a heavy humid darkness was beginning to veil the forest. The powerful jagged trees thrust out and silhouetted against the fading twilight sky, like brutal recriminations ushering in and awakening the distance of solitude. This uncompromising territory occasionally peculiar, always honest and rare. A travellers refuge, where the kind incurious eyes and untrespassing tongues of gentlefolk will pardon and welcome the lost and guileless; and conspire with creation to lend baptismal dew to a hungry heart that hides frightened beneath a self-concealed cryptic smile.

She gentle free wheeled off the road, and by the incandescent glow of the fin lights they hastily gathered their topcoats and a battery powered lamp from the trunk. Squinting into the darkness they began to negotiate the escalating furrowed track through the crowded forest.

'Was this your Pa's old vehicle?' Sandra quirked with uncertainty. They paused, and peered through the rich purple shadows toward a mulch of lamented wild plants and bracken. There entombed lay the semi-skeleton rusted chassis of this treasured 40's Oldsmobile. She drew a deep breath and slowly, respectfully replied, 'El Contessa, that was his sobriquet title for her; we all used to feel so natty riding in her'. She trod carefully, avoiding the narcissus plants (as though they had been recently planted) and culled a tangled twig from the dank vegetation.

Cautiously she prodded at the foliage and the sinewy garland of cobwebs which had grown and threaded like gossamer glass across the companion window aperture. Fastidiously holding her hair away from the mish mash she gingerly peeped through and into the vehicle interior. A distorted breeze of ashen recollections leapt toward her like the crazed reflection of a broken convex mirror. It was impossible but not inconceivable that the pungent fragrance of her mother's jasmine scent still lingered. She realised that its redolence was the deceiving grace of the night shade, merely conspiring with the pulse of her wounded heart. She understood the untrue message of the rancid air: purporting to be subdued and silent, but always watchful, always deluding, muzzled but never mute.

INTERNALIZED CHAPTER 5

The timber built house slumbered like disused lumber on the sheltered South fringe of the forest. By appearance resembling a passé mischance, although in a mellow type of way, perhaps more like a luckless companion who was old by endurance, yet not beyond enduring.

She relaxed lackadaisically upon the feeble porch steps locking her arms neatly around her knees and gazing distantly in Sandra's direction. Sandra was scuffing and squeaking upon a rusty chained swing she had discovered. 'I think I like this place ma'am, it's so cute and magical. Most of all there is no one sneezing or coughing or being horrid". Bringing the swing to an unexpected strident stop and wiping her oxidized hands down her sides, she pointed and declared almost breathlessly, 'See ma'am over yonder, Lucy Montgomery's Tree Lovers'. Poised and huddled around the woodshed each inescapable leafy maple was nesting to her spruce lover; it was as though they had been hiding – seen as children's games and Sandra had tagged them!

INTERNALIZED CHAPTER 6

For the best part of each day, Sandra had the ability to hold an audience far longer and to a greater degree than Kim ever could. Each blasé word had the ability to ripen into euphoria. She had an ironic way of giving a new meaning to sincerity; perhaps because sincerity was the intrinsic part of her, and the salad days she adorned so much. Even here under black moonless branches, she was capable of splashing vibrant patches of rose and lemon, and the illusion of the sheer uncontaminated light of a total summer's day. It was as though she had the knack and virtue to disagree with the dark secrets of the night in her own colloquial fashion, until they capitulated into mere farcical hang dogs.

Its peculiar and curiously puzzling why sometimes we can quite casually be entirely conscious of (and observant too) of an unusual occurrence (or even a phenomenon) without really bothering to be surprised (or alarmed). It was kind of that way when Sandra had unexpectedly arrived in her life. Perhaps the answer (if indeed there was one) was inconsequential and it is not necessary for some secrets to have a notion of explaining themselves. She had recognised from the onset that Sandra had become her perceptive angel, who had the ability to razzle the air with her transparent wings; through which she could often see herself and even her own childhood explained. She had often pondered upon 'love' being the explanation because in any event love is never just an explanation of itself; but nor is true love an emotion. She guessed that perhaps when the unassuming and miraculous are personified and extended into immeasurable clouds of negativity, a soaring flight steadfastly into the positive materialises. When stealthily love becomes the only explanation plausible, it is because of its responsiveness and that its sustenance is as chaste as spring water and Sandra.

INTERNALIZED CHAPTER 7

As the evening began to grow colder, she rose dog eared from the porch steps and began to fastidiously straighten her wrinkled nylons. She had become lost in her own explanations and although she felt that it was time to speak, her mouth had become voiceless. She did not even remember lighting the Camel, it was as though it had grown between her lips and become unconscious. Her imagination was straying, she felt like a bee caught in a honey pot of time and gazing helpless through bifocaled hollow dead silence: across the silver grass and puddles: through the dirt encrusted storm windows laying in the black rain water: she was becoming at one with her hysteria and it was allowing the surreal environment to become the resulting culmination of so many blurred and suffocating nightmares.

Sandra has sensed her clandestine tears and reached out to cradle her damp hands. 'This has been an awesome day ma'am, but I need the bathroom, right now.' Her voice quickened: 'I am not exaggerating, get me the bathroom quick and I promise to always remain your spinster daughter.' Sandra was never predictable, for that matter, she was also never unpredictable; one thing was for sure, her behaviour always essentially contained a good reason. It was the basis of this reason that was the all important motivative factor in her ovative performance. As to suggest whether the so called 'performance' was stunning or hammed; enough to say that Sandra's 'acting' was the natural brightness behind any dark cloud, and that was all that really mattered.

She smiled at Sandra's assertiveness and cautioned with a soft maternal riposte, 'Sandra, you are a genuine heretic, hold on to your pee, think of hockey, ice cream, peanut butter and marshmallow.' She searched frantically through her congested handbag trying to locate the house key. Sandra hooted 'hurry up' and impatiently squirmed and fidgeted with the loose porch handrail.

She fiddled the rusty key into its lock and like stars of a Soviet ballet (in a gesture of total interpretive power) they both forcibly pitched themselves into the swollen front door; falling defiantly through onto the coarse inner mat like dishevelled newspapers with confusing news; and Sandra made her extrasensory run to the bathroom!

INTERNALIZED CHAPTER 8

S omewhere remote, across the room, it glanced positively toward her; a memento of his delirium, its keys twisted and letters faded from the lash of his personal altercation. Now at last retreating in blissful serenity, free from pounding through the labyrinth of his tormented words.

She could still very nearly overhear each personified sharp click, and catch sight of his hunched image; and perceive his rough wool sweater through an embrace.

Brushing the insensitive dust from his chair, she warily sat down; it was as though she needed permission, and he was watchful and evaluating her every move.

The crammed and cluttered bookcases muttered a blank stare solemnly in her direction. Like lost souls seeking delivery and redemption. Each volume had become a narrative of the self-same muted cliché of self-accusation and guilt.

Her father had always been opposed to allowing any volumes whatsoever to be banished to the basement, even for temporary storage; he liked to be encircled by Lincoln, Whitman and Frost and such. 'They are my bastions,' he would say; and they were.

She was amazed and astonished to encounter their ancient piano looking decidedly abandoned and somewhat forlorn in an alcove of the spacious living room. Her father had said that it was only good for firewood because fourteen keys did not work; it was quite possible to stagger through Scarlatti in a strange piercing key in the upper register, but unfortunately Beethoven had always come off rather badly in the base.

INTERNALIZED CHAPTER 9

A fterthoughts are the postscripts which are more significant than the foretold interaction; they are written upon the soul and never completely erased. They are implanted and entombed and become the symbols of imprisonment: outwardly unmentionable, inwardly merciless and malignant. It's always easy to reflect upon the wisdom of hindsight, but fancifully the reality of dreams is merely a lost or abandoned opportunity.

At least his were not afterthoughts, they were pure intolerable wounds. A self-initiating powerless paralysis that evoked the chaos of unread letters, hiding cluttered and fallen around his desk and floor; each individual word squeezed and posted through the aperture of his heart and on through to blind eternity.

She was envious of his thoughts because each one alluded to the throes of losing her; whilst her thoughts of him had become confused and nullified. Albeit, it had been a kind of protection for him to endure his lost hopes and memories. rather than confront his truth. She, on the other hand had been fearful that what she wanted to be true, was not. She refused to chance upon tomorrows truth, for dread it was not as she perceived it to be; it was too great a price to pay when you are unsure.

She had begun to read his thoughts, they had become shared and compatible thoughts. She now understood that his anguish was a curious recompense in disguise. that had made a bargain with his compromised love: his sureness was steadfast, he knew that expectantly and unexpectedly she would return, dutiful and understanding. It was as if she had been his flailing butterfly, afraid and battering at his window of misconception; he had dreamed her home so often, yet could not grasp the unbarred door of conclusion. When finally at last she had flown non-restricted with outstretched arms to his lantern of eternal love it had become a retrospective repatriation.

The questions and the doubt, the solitude and the bitter freedom; a mutual creativity of pathetic tragic self-sacrifice.

The threadbare damp funeral cloths of stained tears had finally dried and been justified. When old tears shed a millennium ago meet unfeigned new tears of happiness, it sometimes becomes a redress of sorts.

The compassionate hazy moon scattered a deep undercurrent of affirmation through the murky chinks of window glass. The journey and the peace of the evening had been reliable and she was indebted and grateful that they had now become hers.

INTERNALIZED CHAPTER 10

T he woodshed was stockpiled with a winter's supply of good dry lumber; in spite of his rather ambivalent manner, her father possessed an extraordinary organised and resourceful disposition.

Like cheery forest foraging creatures they scurried to and fro, gathering and amassing a hoard of sunny logs beside the hearth.

The shutters silenced the sombre after dark and as the fire began to sing and illuminate the room, happy voices cradled and embraced; kindled and warm like long ago. The elderly house was effectually responding and had begun to realise its importance again; it was rejoined and young once more.

Sandra slouched blowsy in the oscillating rocking chair, her toes stretched out toward the fire as far as she dare. From time to time she would rapidly dart them back; it was surely the lesser of two evils: whether to close up to the fire and risk being hit by a fiery spark, or to move out of range and suffer cold feet.

The wavering flames danced wistfully upon their russet faces; the past was painstakingly interlocking with the present, and bringing forward an answer to the undulating future.

There was a delectable, aesthetic mellowness about the evening, like lung warming wine. Beyond the exhaustion of the day, the twilight had arrived unperturbed and easy going.

Sandra puffed eagerly upon her Loblaw's harmonica in an accompaniment to Kim's poetry recital; it was like a recipe for sour cream cookies, once you stir in all the ingredients the blending is astonishingly complementary! Sandra paused momentarily and tapped out the particles of spit from the instrument. She gazed at Sandra endearingly. 'We'll happen on a diner in the morning and have delicious nibbles.' You could almost hear the sparkle in Sandra's eyes: 'Pancakes with butter and syrup... may I have some junk jewellery ma'am; especially for washing in cold water tonight?' she added courageously. Kim smiled and nodded, and tossed another log on the fire.

INTERNALIZED CHAPTER 11

A small wall clock that had been in her mother's family for generations ticked softly in a corner, every passing second a reminder of how far she had come. She gazed mesmerized into the dimming fire and the recollections of her mother came flooding back in sequence: the silly quarrels, the finery of their Sunday clothes, the feel of her soft hair tied back in a knot and falling loose at the days end, the evenings when each laugh was shared.

Sandra was watching her knowingly. 'Please tell me about your mom,' she declared blithely as she pulled the wrap around her. Kim was pleased that Sandra had asked so effortlessly; she gazed into a pause in space and gradually replied, 'Mom made the quilted wrap you're wearing.' Kim had really gone into full explanation flight now: 'She became friends with several German families who had settled here, sometimes they would make a whole quilt in a day.' Kim could tell that Sandra was curious by her puzzled, worrying facial expression: 'Where did they find all the cloth and material?' she asked eagerly. Kim gleamed at her warmly. 'They would use scraps of fabric, maybe my old denim jeans or Dad's old suit, perhaps even some old flour sacks; it was almost a diary of our lives.'

There was an uncomfortable movement over her eyes that felt like tears; she wiped her polished nails across her cheeks and hastily continued: 'Mother was a special woman who knew that her business was to hold things and people together.'

Sandra wailed for a spell on the harmonica; Kim picked thoughtfully at the white cotton brocade on her shawl; she had shown her hardihood, she had defined their self-same name: Krysia Comanescu.

INTERNALIZED CHAPTER 12

A roma from the kerosene lanterns was meandering through every access and recess and saturating the atmosphere with wistful nostalgia... and reassurance that this destination in time had become no less homely than it had ever been.

She was beginning to recognize the reward of contentment again; it had been so long since it had visited her, the sensation felt unreal, almost as if it was the property of another's life.

It washed through her tenderly and overflowed beyond imagination, carrying her to a warm pool of gratification and away from uncertainty. The distance she had travelled had been punishing but the respite was sweet.

The ghosts of yesterday had been waiting in the shadows to rendezvous, but when all she had left was her nakedness, shamefaced they denounced themselves and melted away.

INTERNALIZED CHAPTER 13

The oversized bed creaked and groaned as Sandra snuggled up cosily and safely beside her.

They lie silently and warming together for several minutes, both gazing shiny eyed at the conspicuously large full moon.

Sandra exclaimed that its nose was too big and that its face looked quite plump. Kim replied that the moon looked confused; it was as though it had glimpsed itself as others see it, and somehow that did not fit in with its own conception of itself. Sandra added that the moon was kind, because it had allowed the stars to take up its sky. Kim watched transfixed as a blizzard of galaxies snowed homeward.

THE END

Ode to myself
By Krystyna Comanescu

If tomorrow was yesterday
And next week was now
Should I act different
Or should I just forgive myself?

And if today was tomorrow
And now was even just the beginning of next week
How should I act in my forgiveness?

If forgiveness is what I require for the future
(and the future is hastening near)
Then why can't the past explain itself?

Or perhaps the past was really the beginning of the present
And the present is merely an overtone to the future?

Sometimes it seems that the future has already passed
And has instinctively become the present.

But if I can forgive the past and the present
Can I hope to understand that forgiveness in the future?

Or does my future rely upon
The forgiveness of the present
And the beginning
Of the past?

Return to Limberlost
An epilogue to 'Limberlost'

Chapter One

As if to interpret the significance of warmer weather, the furry snowflakes fell large and lazy throughout the day. It was the first of three long snow days and no colder than a winter Florida morning.

Each journey to the wood shed was surprisingly tedious and inhibited as the snow balled on their feet and the wet flakes festooned their clothing and soaked them in its melt.

The river was high and rising and the swift current clamoured thick and full with floating snow and slush ice.

The end of winter had all the earmarks of another delicate spring in the making: it was as though spring's determination to supersede, was causing winter's last stand fretful pangs of remorse and generally throwing it into disarray.

The furry snow flakes unbatingly descended like eccentric dancing ghosts; this had become winter's swansong, beleaguered and bullied by the unfaltering murmuring of spring's ruffling impatience.

Another morning of another day and like the landscape there are never really endings, only new beginnings: and sometimes unanswered questions and tolerance for unclear reasons: and curiosity for the reasons of improbabilities and the inevitabilities, and the nature of chance.

Chapter Two

'A cotton-candy cry-baby, that's really what I became; and that's all there is to it!'

In fact there was never a precise explanation or indeed a justifiable verdict that could even come close to rationalising the density of Kim's conflict; except to say that perhaps during the course of time she had to an extent discovered her own slant of personal vulnerability, and the antidote to that vulnerability.

The fourteen years of dealing with the past had been a retrospective soul-search that had gradually and gratefully brought about a type of reconcilable understanding; or least-wise a type of 'time-elapsed' post-vindication that she had adjusted to; and learned to live with (if nothing else, make the best of).

In any event the brume that had blighted her essence had miraculously been inclined to move away, extracting with it her charity, faith and hope.

Nowadays Kim lived comparatively happy in her newly acquainted misty bubble, and to all intents she implies an ever so confident and feel-good outlook about her. She was empowered with the ability to 'mood wish' the ragged haunting memories by (if necessary) alternately using and denying them at her own discretion. As apparently they have become her birth right, then decidedly she was in control; the choice was her 'enjoyable' prerogative.

There were occasions when she could become quite pernickety and would literally plan and shape every detail and tiny fragment of her skittish double-barrelled survival. Perhaps because her subtle mind was able to make fine distinctions: or perhaps because (in the most pitiable way) her anguished life had become the honest, heart-rending testimony of a rejected pilgrim seeking the transcendent.

In any event the search would so often meet up with itself and return: like a dark lament that seeks to be light, the merry-go-round would bring her, and take her away; each time more lost and misled.

Always most eloquently and always non-condescending (although historically awkward) she would characteristically and competently toss-off criticism and snipes as though they were merely a nip of her cigarette ash ... though there were often times when those somewhat queasy tumultuous forces invaded (which in the uninspiring night can afflict even the most spunky) the type that will not be appeased or silenced.

But then again, she remembered them from when they visited her some time ago. and she wasn't really so surprised or shocked to see them appear (pretty much on schedule) again.

Sandra however, was an artist at the pinnacle of her craft: A graduate of the University of Michigan, who in spite of opposition, had persistently irked the jowled displeasure from the faculty dean. by absenting her studies each fall. It was her foremost priority to partake the very first sleigh rides with Kim: down and across the virgin snow-covered ridge that formed the cachet of Homestead Hill.

The tranquil, meandering summer vacations were precisely defined as Sandra's primary, to provide amusement and entrainment. She would present a range of concertos and concerto-like compositions from Warsaw Concerto to Clair De Lune: and the front porch podium would rattle and regale at her pianistic passion and vigour. Yonder in the warm gallery, her auspicious audience of tree-softened trilliums beamed with naturalistic ovation.

Her wry wit and 'joie de vivre' were most undeniably fashioned and personified in her music. Times-had-it when Sandra's nigh on jittery pulse of improvisation would virtually change the whole arrangement until it wasn't even close in character to the original sound. Quite out of the blue in her unique adept manor she could carefully blend in her overriding dissimilar, and then unexpectedly swing back gracefully to convention. It had a way of making you question the original composer's competence; or at least cogitate upon his intentions! Perhaps it was because Sandra's derivative was in all respects exceptionally so eccentrically engaging!

Her way of enriching requiems was really a fun-run to behold. She would gather up an accompaniment of thoroughly ebullient words and incorporate them into the existing abysmal chorus.

Like a somewhat bemused funeral parlour guest her engaging eyes would laugh and flare; and even late into the glimmering twilight it was unlikely not to sense her wondrously bountiful smile; detoxifying even the dullest and most bland tune.

Sandra was essentially and always overwhelming, blisteringly infectious: and compelling and buoyant to capacity!

Chapter Three

The sky was without a cloud and the light from the ivory landscape made every leafy branched evergreen look paralysed and as sharp as a blade in the windless air.

Sandra crunched and dallied though the deep snow, full-armed with logs and such from the wood shed, toward their 'chantier' home. Over her shoulder the glass river sparkled and shimmered exuberantly, and the enormous sun cheekily angled down through the branches and threw squinting light at her.

Contemplative at the lattice window, Kim looked up from the brass candlesticks she was polishing and reeled off some chipper encouragement to Sandra's resourcefulness: her voice took on an almost sing-song quality; oftentimes it achieved such resonance. Conceivably it was Kim's idiosyncratic way of plucking a necessity out of a virtue!

The damp lumber was presently hissing and sizzling into blaze like Dante's definition of paradise. It was in every respect an appropriate occasion to discount the calorie rumour, and heartily tuck into poached eggs on buttered whole wheat with beakers of fine quality steamy mocha: at the same time delighting in the watchable bony Fred Astaire 'Flying down to Rio.'

It was only because the commercial had caused them to remember that 'Winston taste good – Like a cigarette should'; and that as a result they accepted the suggestion; and on account of that they invariably converged into a familiar lively Gabfest until around forenoon!

Chapter Four

S andra knew it was time to talk, she knew that it was time to demand Kim's attention. The absolute certainty dwelled in the knowledgeable observation of Kim's frowned expression; and the pleading contained in Kim's eyes.

Sandra had learned to keep tabs on Kim's suppressed loneliness, and was able to observe it lurking in the distance many times before; whereas most folk found it altogether difficult, or down right impossible to outmanoeuvre let alone alleviate any of Kim's 'whimsicals', that came to the fore from time to time. Their intervention was invariably a usefulness of nothing. Sandra's intercession was invariably unique to them both and no one and nothing more besides.

Solely Sandra possessed the empathy to appreciate the 'futures' and the richness of the events that lie ahead, and that Kim was permitted to dream over. And solely Sandra was endowed with the astuteness to realise the 'pasts' and the danger that belonged to a former time; and therefore more usefully buried securely in the vaults of protection.

Sandra eyed her steadily and knowingly:

'I recall back in '63 you were the most exquisitely sophisticated and tasteful dresser in the whole world. Stylistically Jacqueline Kennedy, but with just the right mixture of Holly Golightly.'

Kim smiled warmly and happily at Sandra's canny observation, and showing careful consideration replied:

'I never really addressed myself to the question of style; I tried not to let my vanity fool me.'

She was crowding 40 and had spent too much of her superficial way of living, ducking pointlessly around corners, and throughout in hidey-holes: in order to avoid being regarded or recognised. The whole framework of her life and the sequence of events was the most absurd travesty, and tended to distort and enhance her notoriety even further.

Her thoughts had always felt concerns, and contested in a struggle of muddled confusion over her 'worth'. Aftermost it was becoming increasingly apparent that her anguished heart was also setting about to accede.

Sometimes in a paradoxical tunnel it is blindness not darkness that prevents escape: for it was undoubtedly the state of affairs, that Kim was the only person who could look up into the night sky and never see that the brightest star was indeed herself.

Sandra allowed her head to rest leisurely against Kim's. Her waif's sad eyes strolled in silence through the secret landscape of the blazing logs and beyond.

On all occasions: forever dependably chirpy, Sandra felt inclined to hastily remind

'It was a whole lot of frosty gusts that caused us to come together... and the cream coffee confabs that nourished our attachment...'

Sandra paused briefly as if for once she was at a loss for words:

'Free loading your Camel also helped zillions!' she sassily interjected!

Chapter Five

Maudie Mae McLean

From time to time, as her disposition permitted. Kim had more than a liking to look in on and spend time with her childhood confidant and old time close friend Maudie Mae McLean.

Maudie lay claim to being the proprietress of the nearby village trading post. She was the widow of a migrant Scotsman; and despite that 30 years (or more) had amassed since his demise even now Maudie carried on with the business.

By all accounts she had quite an illustrious ancestry. in fact it is proven that she boasted direct lineage to the great chief Joseph.

Rumour has it that during 1878 when Joseph and the Nez Perc´e were captured. his daughter and grandchild were part of a small group who skipped undetected through the army's lines, and into the sanctuary of neutral Canada.

Kim and Maudie possessed extremely like-minded souls; more so than purely a rapport; it was to a greater extent more like an affinity or a kinship.

They both really loved to shoot the breeze; and there was a so pleasant reciprocal determination to enthuse and enthral over each and every bit of casual conversation.

Kim was especially absorbed by Maudie's graphic and potent narratives, that connected with Indian culture and ancient traditions: in particular her folklore tales of myth and legend.

Oddly enough, in many respects much of this mythology encompasses a resounding credibility: that happens to be an explanatory, not dissimilar to the unwelcome grimaces that abide in the so-called 'real world' of Kim's draconian labyrinth. In as much that it is inclined to be: often threatening, usually quite bizarre and frequently inhabited by uncanny beings and the most inexplicable phenomena.

American Indians belief acknowledged that in order to make sense of the unpredictable universe, it was first necessary to understand the past. Indeed, in order to attempt an explanation of the present, it was first necessary to visit the past.

Explicitly: when danger is not well lit and hunches have become undependable: when the crossroads has become infected and double-dealed, and fate itself has lost its direction... the sign of things to come can be found by following the road signs back to the beginning.

Chapter Six

Perhaps once in a while there really could have been 'new beginnings' for Kim: she had indeed attempted to return to that elusive past beginning, subconsciously trusting Homestead Hill to provide her with the answers she sought, or in any event, to at least offer her a reasonable explanation.

The reality and the falsehood of such a flight of fancy consisted of nothing much more than a world which had returned in to itself: and much of the same smudged perceptions and imageless horrors, and consistently the same mute scream for love.

Homestead Hill was not the guardian of the truth that it had appertained itself to be, nor was it the optimistic discovery and notion of liberty that she pertained to it: In fact Homestead Hill was as much a prisoner of melancholy as she was.

Its irresistible presence dominating and punishing her. It was as though she was a broken china doll that Homestead Hill had found and rescued: but how difficult it had become for them to find a peaceful co-existence with themselves, unless she submitted to becoming crushed and silent in their presence.

From time to time when her fatalism unexpectedly dwindled, she had the dexterity to randomly select and call on some nostalgic sentiment associated with the past: for the purpose of blanking out the dark residue of reality that permeated the present.

Despite that there were very few of these sentiments left in reserve - for by definition of their usefulness, most now had the ability to surgically dissect from her memory and implode to dust in her heart.

Chapter Seven

However, there had been one particular special summer; a peculiar summer; a summer of the most unlikely beginnings; a summer that had helped her to survive.

With every cool green perfumed morning of blossom on the breeze; and each pure white sublime day, that wanted too and felt they could infinitely stay. The crimson taste and ripe aroma of the vegetation at dusk and at nightfall the heavy ebony branches smeared with moonlit silver, and the bullfrogs kvetching in the shadowy crick.

And the gentle folk who had evoked her aspirations and expectations, and allowed her to freely peel off her restraints to become visible and freed.

An amalgamate of dreamscaped events that quite unexpectedly discovered themselves at an outpost en route to anywhere; and yet quite significantly remained vitreously clear in her memory and established a place in her heart.

In somewhat tongue tied confusion she browsed through the plangent pages of her journal; not a word or pen stroke had changed in fourteen years: she was still so thirsty for the scents and for the laughter; and couldn't help question her rational for running away.

Maybe it was because of, at that stage the resume of her entire life was still raw and consequently it was still in a violent struggle to express itself as darkness: and now perhaps her unblinking eyes had become adjusted to such, and capable of accepting the compassionate gift on offer. Like some frightened foraging creature, she had chosen to skedaddle and to bury the secret in the abyss of her deranged logic; rather than risk a new encounter.

But now she desperately wanted that new beginning. She had turned once, twice, and maybe three times; and she knew for certain that she was ready, and that she couldn't live without its promise any longer.

Kim closed her journal without sentence or speech as though it contained the reconcilable enlightenment of past errors. Acceptance, was undoubtedly the intimate she had been searching for, and there was so much more to seeing it than merely looking at it or whispering down her breath to it in desire.

Valley Forge Trading Post
Homestead Hill
May 21/78

My Krystyna,

Quietly I am tending you my thoughts: you are knowing of our way to
see the unseen by means of deep silence.

I recall, when as a little one, you were fond of plucking the red
cardinals that were hidden by the snow: you told me that the silent
voice of the mountain trees had 'sneaked' on the flowers and made
them visible to you.

Gather your thoughts once more Krystyna and see in your silence that
the ice on the lake is slowly melting, and the night snow is turning to
drizzle; and despite spring interfering it is still cold.

Johnny Appleseed[5] has dropped behind and put forth shoots for you;
and moreover Coyote[6] knows your admiration and will not suffice
your soul or harbour your lodge at any time forevermore.

As one, Maudie Mae

---

[5] Johnny Appleseed: Spiritual vanguard to Indians.

[6] Coyote (or Sedet): embodies the destructive aspects of human emotion.

Chapter Eight

'So long old ugly house.'

Just moments before the ambivalence of daylight finally decided to reveal its concealed impurities, and just before the mantel clock interrupted startlingly, with its iterated chime-in: the daybreak paused briefly in order to allow the sun an interval to gather its strength.

It was a dawn so silently audible that the tiniest globs of dew could be heard falling insidiously to earth; and even the distant sad howl of a loveless hound did little to alleviate the total tranquillity.

The age old conflict between the end of winter and the illusion of spring was over, and abruptly the reality of an aspiring summer had begun: devotedly, the sultry forest was in turn responding.

Eager tenderfoot buds were rousing and merging into a hundred heavenly trinities of beauteous blossoming colour, and in and around every nook and cranny the warm bosky undergrowth thickened and tangled impenetrably.

By the time that sunup had obliged their quirky shadows to grow fat, the echo of giggly enlivened voices vibrated through the woodland; and earnest sprightly feet scuttled toward town: it was the most exceptional daybreak when Kim and Sandra left Homestead Hill.

Chapter Nine

There was a peculiar unearthly splendour and serenity that propagated the early morning tone of the township.

Although the farming populace had been up for hours, most folks were still sleeping in the upscale municipal district.

Nevertheless there was an uneasy awareness that secretly from behind some rustling curtain. your every step was being witnessed and evaluated.

Perhaps a somewhat more logical and comprehensive explanation would be Sandra's diabolical shocking red polka dot dress aligned with Kim's self-appointed paranoia.

Their Greyhound rested wearily by the wayside, parked up under a long enduring oak tree; across the thoroughfare in O.J. Baileys Diner. the gaunt driver coughed his route through broiled ham and eggs.

O.J. was a masterful schmoozer and was always willing to initiate a conversation (particularly if he discerned that he may gain an advantage!) O.J. was confident that he had arised the driver's irritation by his adversary's 'screech owl' response. The point of contention was over Carter's Presidential Pardon of Vietnam era draft evaders and Canada's involvement in such: but by and large it was an ordinary morning like any other.

Chapter Ten

Like a shambling creek toad, the detached driver burped his entry back onto the bus; and as if in sympathy with his digestion the reawakened vehicle jerked and lurched in short spurts all the way down Main Street.

The weather outside was magnificent: the sky cloudless, pure blue on blue and not breathing.

Kim sat upright and expectant, looking out inquisitively from every window; her large lustrous eyes saying more than the spoken word could ever manage.

Sandra was slouched mawkishly with her cheek pressed rumly against the window; her eyes nonchalantly catching life as it inimitably passed by. Each person discretely filled with their own unique animated perspective and enjoying the chipper bouncing scenery.

This farming country: fresh turned chocolate earth, and crops that spill endlessly across the province: a place so splendid that even the birds float with dignity over the newly planted fields.

Drowsy trees woofed fleetingly past the windows, each pot hole, each gliding motion a voyage of re-flourished imagining and urgency.

The sensation of leaving had given her a dizzy-rush, a joy that she had never experienced before; or had even dared to suspect. Indeed, although she had not chosen this May 'birth' she was nevertheless truly grateful that it incredulously had chosen her.

The warming winds and warmer thoughts of warmer climes. The smell of dried hay and some other peculiar sweet scent, (which she surmised may be tobacco crops) it was all within her grasp.

She wanted to reveal her new found excitement and express her deep gratitude to Sandra: who was always in the habit of being so strong; who could always see behind even the most vaguest star. However somewhere in the jungle of history was a cause that made it difficult to allow such intimate secrets to be seen just yet.

She had made so many superficial journeys in the past that the profanity of a Greyhound excursion to utopia, may be a somewhat difficult scenario to explain. Even to herself, it was perplexing to comprehend.

Chapter Eleven

The exhausted archaic bus drifted slowly and lazily through the rural backwoods toward Anville.

Each village seemed smaller and less undisturbed than the one before: each mile past seemed closer between the wanting and the doing.

Kim was still holding firm to the dependability of her predetermined innate pessimism: it was similar to some old sweater with holes in it; you want to throw it away but somehow you still need it. Old habits tend to die hard, especially in view of the fact that she had at least a bucket load of them.

Unwearyingly Kim had become the perfect personification of her own clichéd habits, and furthermore the contradiction of her so-called heart-set coveting.

It had always been her custom to hotfoot away, to escape and become invisible: but strangely enough, although she had previously been captive to these thoughts, it was not in any regard comparable to now. For once, on this occasion, she had a yearning to stay put.

Such conflicting Catch 22 emotions: Kim was strong yet vulnerable; neither approving nor disapproving of herself. Fallaciously she had begun to convince her intellect of the necessity to experience total nothingness; she was no stranger to that anxiety.

Stepping down from the bus on the outskirt fringes of Anville, they set about an 'aroused' three mile march to 'Limberlost'.

They were both beginning to display identical uncontrolled peculiarities; it was as though they had disembarked hand in hand on the same cloud 9!

Jointly enlivened and intoxicated by similar unintelligible thoughts and behaviour, and brimming over with inconsequential silly, beautiful triflings: Sandra chuntered on and on overmuch about how, metaphorically they had 'hopped a freight train': Kim skipped from one foot to the other, splashing and baptising her feet and ankles in every roadside puddle she could find. There was a wealth of love, affection and manic laughter between them; and particular amusement over Kim's need of spectacles.

The bridge to the moon was fragilely built and daunting; it needed the sustenance of so-giddy repartee to tease and to lighten the footsteps across; to justly reach the other side.

Chapter Twelve

A soft glowing deep purple hue spectacularly absorbed the twilight air as the radiant sun silently melted below the horizon.

The distant red maples were dazzlingly metamorphosising to scarlet bright against the cold green pines.

It was that mesmerising decline of the day when the human spirit clearly wears the suited optimism of nature: when even the most opaque objects become transparent.

'Mourning in the glade'

'Limberlost' forlornly neglected and dejected: an uninhabited 'Brigadoon': a vision of invisibility, planted and hidden in a boondocks of dense vegetation and brambles: taunted by tumbleweed and unable or unwilling to cry out: its exclusive credentials, a haphazardly nailed 'Realty' sign swinging from the soffit.

Sandra had more than a notion that unknown responsive words were in Kim's throat and Kim was eager to speak them.

Kim raked her fingers thoughtfully through her hair. there was a surprising calmness in her voice

'You know sweetie-pie. I am really goin' to get my fortune told next time, before I get all dressed up like some chocolate dog.'

Sandra half smiled, it was as though her feistiness was confused. She had unfailingly always been most capable of perceiving and feeling the sting of Kim's disappointment and pain; in this circumstance she whole heartedly shared it with Kim.

She wiped the wetness from the corners of her eyes.

'It's not what we've found here today ma'am it's what we dream it 'can' be.'

Whatever changes under the skin is a secret that sometimes fortunately no-one sees. People smile when they don't smile, people cry when they don't cry; and reality is only really what we imagine, speculate or observe it to be.

Kim was never the guardian of such chicanery and monkey-shines: her face and body always illustrated the complete truth; quite clearly and quite unequivocally.

She accepted and was content that her life was destined to be cut short by heartache, by grief, by mistakes, by guilt, by shame; but never by her emotion. That would never be a compromised companion; she would never allow herself to become numb!

Her trembling manicured hands tore and rattled the impudent rusty padlocked front door until it snapped open and broke!

Chapter Thirteen

L ike a dark deserted underpass the neglected diner sprawled out uninspiringly beyond sight and seemingly into nowhere.

Only the swarthy silence was conspicuous; it was as though their abrupt arrival had irreverently dislodged its orientation: and now it stared back at them intently.

The semblance of life was being initiated by a solitary drip-drop of some leaking conduit: strangely enough it was a very welcome sound.

For a moment or two, headlights from the highway interrupted the dead panned shadows that skulked across the lobby: now here, now there, now gone; into well-nigh invisibility and back to their hide-away again.

By and by they became mindful that their eyes had begun to defeat the darkness and that there had become a comfortable abidance: inasmuch that every hushed decibel and orphaned reverberation in the restaurant was stirring and warming to their presence; as if every element had been held in limbo, waiting patiently for the door of opportunity to open and reward them.

Loitering forlorn in the inkiest most cobwebbed corner of the dairy bar, the stout Wurlitzer was credibly beginning to breath a new pulse of 'bop' inside its Bakelite jacket: quietly and discretely with sober excitement.

Chapter Fourteen

I n such circumstances where Kim's fortitude had dwindled; and emotionally she had arrived at the particular place beyond which no more can be absorbed: she oftentimes became aware of her mother's characteristic scent. Kim figured it was something of a warning, but in any event it was singularly her occurrence and no-one more besides.

In contrast, this time it came like a compassionate breeze; touching and unwrapping every tight little knot of uncertainty: this time its articulation was precise.

Thoughtfully with a sense of purpose the delicate air of jasmine meandered through the dimsicle light of transition and into new resolutions.

Every tectonic plate of solution calmed and settled; the elusive explanation nakedly revealed and the unjustifiable vindicated.

Be all that as it may, it was still extremely difficult for Kim to comprehend a rendezvous of such practicable common sense and fantasy: it was similar in nature to unravelling a dream in its entirety and waking to find strange bedfellows with an untypical surreal pragmatism!

Materialising (slightly dithery) from her thoughts she stammered and stumbled:

'Sweetie-pie I owe you and my mother a much better smile than the one I put on to go out into the cold: anyway what possible new excuses could I make not to smile even to myself.'

Aiming a pointing finger toward the juke box in a snarky, zany manor appropriate to a child she twittered:

'Waiting tables, filling up a theatre, you imagined that maybe you'd seen the last of me: but bear in mind I haven't forgotten that you still owe me a quarter!'

Chapter Fifteen

The Homecoming...

Serendipitous circumstance had meticulously tracked her down and encircled her; but perhaps it should be said that by nature she had been intuitively drawn towards its ethereal value: that had made it impossible for her not to take its outstretched hand.

Although it had transpired that Limberlost was undoubtedly far more than a happenstance of fate; it was nonetheless quite the most unlikely foretoken of Eldorado...

And; unsurpassably beguiling to ever contemplate the sight of Sandra garbed in a floppy chef's hat and Kim warbling like a demented blue jay (in total emancipation) over hot sizzling succotash!

Winter Creek was very nearly down to its summer level, before the hazy shadow of its luke water and the moon's wavering image were awakened by neon light: and happy-go-lucky voices caressed the balmy night air: and deliverance was procured, whole and entire.

Kim's dream of home was a state of mind and it had always been the answer to the question that she had become frightened to ask. When; in a gradual way, she discovered it was simpler to steadily acknowledge the 'existence' of the question; did the honesty of her innocence prevail; and the vulnerability of her sadness eventually chaperone her home.

The End

Limberlost

.... A creek meanders around a gentle bend
   Bringing what was into focus

.... A small shanty with peaked rooftops
   Bringing a memory closer to reality

.... A journey to another time
   Bringing a heart warmth.

We live with the nearness of our past.

Remember ....

Krystyna Comanescu

A NOTE ABOUT THE AUTHOR

Ricky Dale was born in England and raised in West Africa and North America; his mother referred to the family as being of 'Colonial' nationality.

Ricky's singing career began in 1959 with one-nighters, college dates, and the occasional radio show.

As fame increased, he began to- and fro-ing across the Atlantic: giving pleasure to capacity audiences in clubs and theatres.

An individual style and heartfelt rendering of ballads, and the contrast of his wild Rock 'n Roll were, he says, 'Inspired from the hope and energy of West Africa.'

As the 60's developed Ricky began to shun the glare of celebrity. Studios, clubs, and stages pulsed with drugs: and a tragic mass entertainment of messed-up, so-called music was becoming mainstream. After a long absence from the stage, he completed contractual obligations in Niagara and Southampton, England and literally faded into obscurity.

In 2000 Ricky, with his daughter Kim, visited Canada. 'It was a kind of odyssey to the past,' he says.

Their poignant journey encompassed the Brant Inn location in Burlington, Ontario.

Decades before, as an enterprising teenager from England, he stepped into the limelight of this fabulous nightclub and truly perfected his craft.

In that golden era a host of glamorous stars entertained the Brant's sophisticated audiences. Ricky had fronted the Guy Lombardo Band, duetted with the sheer genius Danny Kaye, and had been 'mothered' by the beautiful Jayne Mansfield: 'When the old-timers were mean to me, she provided sympathetic company where I could escape at will and complain.'

'The Brant Inn was tragically torn down in around 1970; but as Kim and I stood on the shore of Lake Ontario (near Maple Avenue), we could easily imagine the melodies that had floated out across the lake: sometimes reality is not permitted to be an intruder!'

Ricky was MD of several innovative companies in the West of England for 21 years.

He now divides his time between his children and his writing.

CPSIA information can be obtained at www.ICGtesting.com
Printed in the USA
LVOW06s1959130813

347707LV00002B/710/P

9 781908 026132